HESKET

SARA BAYAT

HESKET
A NORFOLK HAUNTING

corsair

CORSAIR

First published in Great Britain in 2026 by Corsair

1 3 5 7 9 10 8 6 4 2

Copyright © Sara Bayat, 2026
Map illustration copyright © Ben Hunt, 2026

The moral right of the author has been asserted.

*All characters and events in this publication, other than those
clearly in the public domain, are fictitious and any resemblance
to real persons, living or dead, is purely coincidental.*

All rights reserved.
No part of this publication may be reproduced, stored in a
retrieval system, or transmitted, in any form or by any means, without
the prior permission in writing of the publisher, nor be otherwise circulated
in any form of binding or cover other than that in which it is published
and without a similar condition including this condition being
imposed on the subsequent purchaser.

A CIP catalogue record for this book
is available from the British Library.

Hardback ISBN: 978-1-4721-6003-4

Typeset in Warnock by M Rules
Printed and bound in Great Britain by Clays Ltd, Elcograf S.p.A.

Papers used by Corsair are from well-managed forests
and other responsible sources.

Corsair	The authorised representative
An imprint of	in the EEA is
Little, Brown Book Group	Hachette Ireland
Carmelite House	8 Castlecourt Centre
50 Victoria Embankment	Dublin 15, D15 XTP3, Ireland
London EC4Y 0DZ	(email: info@hbgi.ie)

An Hachette UK Company
www.hachette.co.uk

www.littlebrown.co.uk

For my family

Prologue	1
Isla	5
Rio	38
Nell	63
Jack	88
Finn	117
Emir	144
Rev. Eileen	174
Arthur	198
Epilogue	221

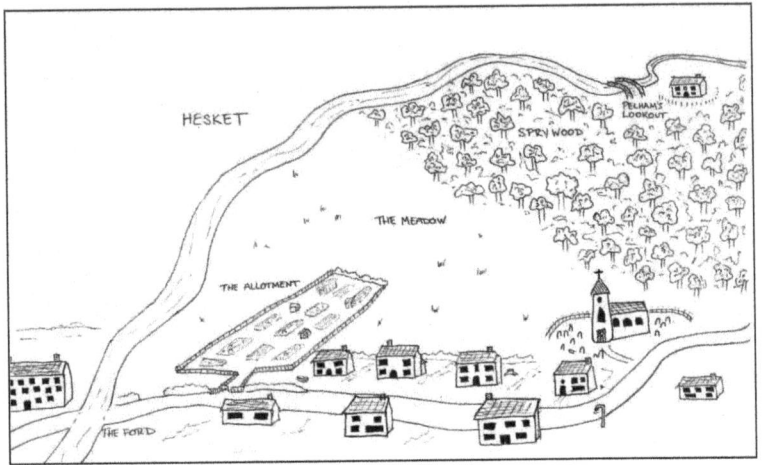

Prologue

1647

On the River Wensum in Norfolk, where the water winds wide and slow around the village of Hesket, Alice Spry is accused of having the marks of a witch, one on her neck, another on her ribs: teats to suckle the devil's imps; only moles she has had since birth, no different than anyone else.

She's been witnessed cavorting with her familiar, a toad, by moonlight, even though she thinks toads vile, and their swollen folds of warty skin elicit revulsion in her.

She's charged with bewitching the poor Filby child, who was menaced by strange fits, the convulsions continuing for days until death, so says the boy's uncle. Only a fortnight before, she peeled the boy an apple from the precious few she'd managed to save. She'd been a young widow then, surviving on parish handouts, and now she is a witch.

Such is the power stories hold, that flights of imagination are turned into truths, and like the eight women who had gone before her (some of whom were her friends, most she has known since infancy), her wrists are to be bound tightly to her ankles so that she's rounded like a stone, and undergo a trial by water. If she floats, she'll be hanged by the neck until dead.

Her protestations that it isn't a fair test, that she cannot swim, are met with jeers from the gathered crowd. Even the women look at her with fear. She catches the eye of her neighbour, John Blofield, who used to stop at her window and tell jokes, and pleads for his help. He spits at her.

The water, when they throw her in, is so cold that it steals her breath before she can gulp it; not more than a second and she is submerged. The last thing she glimpses before going under are the oak trees swaying along the river's edge.

Terror as she sinks, as the voices on the bank are muted by the river pulsing and bubbling around her. Her hands are desperate to find purchase but grasp only water; trembling branches of oak reach across the thin light above – if only she can stretch out her arm and pull herself up the way she did as a child, determined to climb every tree in the woods. She struggles, thrashing like a pike on a line, but the rope shackling her limbs to one another is resolute and doesn't give, and all she can do is flail her legs uselessly, the movement nearly wrenching her arms from their sockets. Her lungs burn; she has to fight the impulse to inhale. The weight of her sodden clothes is painful. When her lungs give out, she swallows river, the taste of it fishy, clogging her throat. She's dizzy. Her vision spots. She sees the branches far above tremble and shimmer, then curve downward like the neck of a swan and dip into the water, wooden fingers elongating through the murk, coming to cradle her, to free her, and she is a girl again, a wisp, no longer afraid as a canopy of oak leaves surrounds her, and the water is light as air, and she is no longer in her body.

Isla

2025

Thinking on it now, it seemed the kind of thing unlikely to have been real, a figment of those first delirious months of parenthood. She can remember vividly how it began, with pitches of static over the baby monitor clipped to her belt while she hung sleepsuits and muslins on the line to dry, the interference becoming gradually more solid, as if the monitor had picked up a radio station and, with it, the dissonant drone of a string section warming up before the music.

Isla had gone to Daniel with it, found him in the kitchen with his ear against the fridge, sandwiches half-made on the counter behind him. 'Do you hear that humming?' he said. 'I can't tell where it's coming from.'

'I'm going to check if it's a problem with the monitor,' she replied. But the sound was layered now: sharp buzzing waves from the device in her hand mixed with a duller, steadier harmony from another room.

He looked confused and took the monitor from her, listening. 'Doesn't it sound a lot like—'

'Is it upstairs?' In those seconds before panic set in.

The baby.

Daniel was faster than her, could vault up the steps three at a time, and was bursting open the nursery door as she crested the top stair, the noise now so shrill and so clamorous it vibrated in her ear canal (such a loudness from things so small), and she could see the turbid heaviness of bees as Daniel hurried to the crib – hundreds of them, thousands – clouding above it like a living mobile, and her little Molly burbling, unbothered that they were crawling on the soft flesh of her belly, her kicking, bare legs (a foreshadowing, Isla would think years later, of the disorder that would menace their daughter throughout her life). It was Daniel they stung as he lifted Molly away from the swarm, as if he were the danger and not them, and to this day Isla doesn't know if the smell, like burned honey and smoke, was something she imagined, as though the agitation of thousands of tiny wings caused a friction in the room. Later, the beekeeper discovered they'd chewed through the dry wall just above the skirting, likely looking for a new place to nest, he said, but how strange it was for a hive to do so like that, to swarm without a queen.

Isla was sat alone at the table with the *Norfolk Times* spread before her. Mornings were like this now, no longer unceremoniously stood at the sink inhaling toast as she prepared school lunch and plaited her daughter's hair, and said things like, *If I take half the gold coins from a treasure chest and you take a quarter of the coins and there's three coins left, how many were at the start?* And *how do you spell 'attached'?* Instead, they were spent quietly sipping a mug of piping coffee as she browsed the newspaper; rarely did she eat breakfast anymore.

She licked her finger to turn the page at its corner, and there at the bottom, crammed in like an afterthought, she read the announcement for the first time, was shocked by both its contents and the immediacy with which a roiling dread filled her, and she thought then – she didn't quite know why – of having to steady herself against the sink and spit into the basin to stop herself vomiting.

When Isla was pregnant the nausea was draining, perpetual. She tried sucking on boiled ginger sweets but the smell turned her stomach, or she'd sip peppermint tea and gag. Daniel fed her salted crackers a nibble at a time, plain boiled rice in portions the size of a soy sauce ramekin. The only thing that soothed her sickness was soil; the urge for it had been overwhelming, the relief it gave immediate. Her doctor said it was a condition called pica and was nothing to be concerned about, that it was simply a sign of mineral deficiency, and that a little dirt now and then never hurt anyone. Her blood was taken, calcium and iron increased. But even after the morning sickness had gone completely, she'd allow herself to taste a small mound in the flower bed each day, enjoyed the act of licking her finger and dipping the whole of it in, coating her mouth with it; sun-warmed sometimes, cool and damp at others. She found that soil from different locations had its own distinct flavour: they drove to the coast in her second trimester and the soil along the cliff fizzed in her mouth like sour sweets, a sharp citrus taste that made Molly kick. From the meadow behind their house, it tasted fresh like rain, while at the entrance to Spry Wood it was sandy and bland, and further in near the river where it felt silty on her tongue it was almost sweet, chocolatey. But the best was licked from underneath moss, flavoured the way the air smells on a hot day right after a downpour, like the shatterings of a late July thunderstorm.

But that was years ago now, nearly a decade gone.

In the garden, she stood at the lean-to with the newspaper under her arm and cupped her hand to textured glass that rippled like wind along a river. She could just make out the fuzzy shape of Daniel bent over the drafting table, the upright structure of his easel behind him, could see the vivid squares of the Werner's Nomenclature poster pinned on the wall. Knocking tentatively, she waited for him to finish whatever he was doing. Isla bought Daniel the nomenclature poster – depicting 110 colours identified by Werner with corresponding examples found in nature – from a museum when they'd lived in London and not been dating more than a few months. She'd picked it up on impulse and then debated for hours as to whether to even give it him, because what's sexy about the classification of colour in the natural world. But of all the presents she'd got him since, it remained his most used, his most enjoyed. Daniel was a botanical and natural science illustrator, mostly freelance commissions for textbooks or species identification guides, but also things like jam labels and artisan greeting cards. His work involved intricate diagrams of small things made big – the anatomy of a seed or bluebottle – and big things made small, like the various parts of an oak tree. His illustrations were delicate and lifelike, carefully considered in either watercolour or acrylic, or sometimes coloured pencil. When he worked (which was something he'd not done much of over the last year, had only recently started doing again in small bits), it was here in the lean-to, a place she wasn't allowed unless invited because recreating accurate minutiae requires concentration. This was implied by the lock on the door, which was once for keeping small fingers out of the paint when no one was looking, but these days could only be for her.

Scattered kernels of uneaten birdseed had sprouted into wheat on the lawn long before the drought arrived, and since she'd mown it back, there were now severed yellow stalks that poked through her tights and itched at her ankles. It was nearing the end of July now, and there'd still been no rain. Breath curled faintly from her mouth in the early-morning chill, and she didn't allow herself to linger on the thought of school runs in the cold, when they'd pretended to be dragons roaring smoke in each other's faces. She pulled her cardigan down over her hands and saw a small hole in one of the sleeves that she'd forgotten was there, moth eaten.

Finally, the slow scrape of Daniel's chair was followed by his pixellated face at the glass, the key turning.

'Why do you still lock it?' she said as it swung open.

'Sorry.' He smiled, boyish, despite the stubble and the dark smudges beneath his eyes, which were both Imperial Purple, like the deep parts of a saffron crocus, and Greyish Blue, the back of a blue titmouse. 'Old habits, love.'

She peered past him, hoping for a glimpse of what he was working on for Geraldine; there was always a sample that he drew from – a leaf, a flower stem in a glass of water, a pin-mounted cricket loaned from some collection – but the room gave nothing away.

She was aware that he was waiting for her to explain the interruption, but what she'd come to tell him didn't feel tangible, was too appalling to possibly be real, and so in the short walk from the kitchen to here, she had convinced herself that she'd misunderstood and that he'd question why she even disturbed him in the first place, with this article that would certainly be about nothing important. She pulled the newspaper from the crook of her elbow and held it out to him.

'What is it?'

She shook her head.

'Isla,' he said. 'What?'

'I must be mistaken.'

She watched him read it, watched his cheeks flatten, his eyebrows slope. So it was true, after all. 'A housing development?' he whispered, raising his hand to his mouth. The panic, the anger; all of it held in his face. 'But it's our woods.' He sounded dazed, faraway. 'They can't cut it down.'

Our. She knew that he did not mean her.

Threat hung over the village like a rain cloud: the development was all anyone talked about when they stopped her in the street to chat; Paul from up the road said that spirits on the allotment had become subdued. The vicar, Rev. Eileen Wright, organised a community meeting at the church, which was attended by everyone, including some residents of the neighbouring hamlets. The sale of the land had been too quiet and abrupt, which gave it the air of being underhand; no one knew when the surveyors had made their assessments. A public consultation was held for twenty-one days, and though residents of Hesket refuted the proposal, the project was given the green light anyway and the whole thing was fast-tracked, which made everyone think that the consultation had only been for show and the council never had any intention of halting the plans from going ahead. The development company, Caldwell & Associates, sent round a pamphlet which promised they would not cull the entirety of Spry Wood. To build their luxury homes, they would concentrate on woodland nearest the river, leaving the other third intact for privacy (and, it was speculated, to separate them from the rest of the village chaff). Where possible, they would leave the most ancient trees standing on the development site if they were structurally sound and visually pleasing, or had a protection order due to roosting bats. They would lay an asphalt road through the meadow for access, and within a few years, more affordable housing and retail spaces would be constructed along it. They cited village and economic expansion as one of the many benefits, the addition of a tennis court and even, in time, a small golf course. There would still be pockets of meadow and woodland left for aesthetic appeal, though these would now be private land.

A petition opposing the project was sent round citing a strain on infrastructure, increased traffic, loss of rural character and property devaluation, not to mention that it would be detrimental to the local ecology. There were worries that the build would create noise and waste pollution, and that the loss of the woods would be historically significant too, given that they'd been named after the last woman in Hesket to be accused of witchcraft.

Daniel had taken to sleeping, drifting between the bed and the sofa, as if the weight of his despondency was too exhausting to remain upright for long. Come late August, he roused himself enough to make various posters on sheets of A4 and showed them to Isla.

SPRY WOOD
HAS THE RIGHT
TO LIVE

and

DON'T PERSECUTE
OUR TREES!

She helped him tack the posters to their windows and door, and to every pole along the road and the bulletin board at the old church, at the entrance to every pathway worn into the woods, slotted them through each letterbox from the top of the village and down to the ford – The Splash, Molly had called it – where the road dipped and the river washed across it four inches or so deep (though it was shallower these days. It was a wonder there was anything at all, with the drought).

'We need more.' Daniel was already marching home. 'They should be everywhere for at least a ten-mile radius.'

'We'll go out at the weekend,' Isla agreed. 'See if anyone can help get them up.'

'No,' he said, 'I'll do it tomorrow. The sooner they're up, the better.'

'But it'll take you days if you go alone. You've the commission for Geraldine to do.'

'I think this is the priority, Isla.' A coldness in the way he said it, and then, 'Molly would be devastated.'

It was the last part that stopped her. As if she wasn't already aware, as if she didn't already feel it keenly. 'I know she would. Do you think I don't *know* that?'

His pace didn't even falter.

She sometimes imagined that he greedily believed himself to be alone in this pain when it was the two of them suffering, as if he'd forgotten it's a mother who first and most tangibly bears the agony of children, who acutely understands emptying, a loss from within. It had been complications of Molly's seizures that took her – an apnea that lasted too long, the muscles in her chest too contracted for her to breathe properly, so that her little body stiffened and lurched horrifyingly, spine so arched she looked about to levitate from the floor, eyes rolling back in her head, lips blue.

Isla would not follow him home, not right away, and sat

instead against a low stone wall in front of one of the houses, her legs stretched out on the pavement in front of her like a doll. It was obvious what he was doing, how he was concentrating his grief on the loss of the woods, and even though he'd wounded her she understood it, the need for it to go somewhere else, if only for a little while, to get it out of you somehow. She channelled hers into work.

Five years ago, Geraldine had resurrected her grandparents' small press, Lantern Books, out of her attic, and published titles like, *The A–Z Guide to Norfolk* and *The Broads by Foot: A Pilgrimage of East Anglian Rivers*. Isla worked mainly as Geraldine's editor, while Geraldine handled research, marketing and online sales. Geraldine's wife, Nat, took care of the bookkeeping and morale, which meant that she spent most of her day downstairs listening to true crime podcasts and bringing up trays of coffee or fruit salad. Isla had managed to persuade Geraldine to give the cover art commission for their latest project, *A Miscellany of Strange Norfolk*, to Daniel, had assured her that he was up to the job. It had been kind of Geraldine to agree; she knew how badly they needed the money, how long Isla had been the only one between them earning, that they'd been living hand to mouth. Isla wondered in that moment if he was going to let her down, if she would have to admit this much to Geraldine, and then, loyally, despite how he'd just behaved, she told herself he'd done more with less time.

He used to show her his work unprompted, proud and earnest and unsure of it, and see if she and Molly could guess his colours according to Werner's chart. The petal tip of an orange marigold he was working on, for example, might be nearest to what Werner called Orpiment Orange (see also: the belly of a warty newt; an Indian cress flower), with a touch of Deep Reddish Orange (goldfish lustre abstracted; a Scarlet Leadington apple). The game wasn't limited to what was on the easel; Molly collected bits from around the garden to present at the lean-to door. Things small enough to pocket would be carefully and dutifully carried home from school or roadside verges, their weekend rambles. To retrieve Werner's colours from the well of her memory was an instinct Isla had not yet lost: a hedge outside Geraldine's house could be Sap Green or Wax Yellow depending on the light that day, while the postwoman's bag was Aurora Red. *Are you sure?* she could sometimes hear Molly say. *Are you sure it isn't something else?*

The pavement beneath Isla's jeans was cool enough that she thought it might be damp, though when she put her palm against it to check, she found it was bone dry. A yellowed leaf skipped along in the breeze; Daniel told her that because of the drought, the trees around Hesket were stressed and shedding their leaves in an attempt to conserve water and energy, entering themselves into a false autumn to survive.

He was likely home now, printing off more posters. From somewhere near a bird was singing, the sharpness of its sound seeming almost to trill all around and within her. Isla closed her eyes to stop herself crying. How had she ended up in Hesket, a village so small it fit entirely within a hollow on the edge of a river, and had only houses, an allotment, a church, a single streetlight and a retirement home for the elderly, but no shop or café, not even a pub? A nowhere place. It had been affordable because of its lack of amenities and draughty old houses, so she'd not put up much protest when Daniel had argued it was the best kind of home for a family to settle, close to nature.

But why were they still here?

'Are you dead, young lady, or just asleep?'

Isla opened her eyes. Ms Riley was peering down at her, smiling cheekily; she had white hair and long, yellow teeth like a rodent, and was small in the way that age shrinks, though this wasn't helped by the woollen coat she wore, the Pearl Grey of a gull's back, which was far too large for her.

'I shouldn't be sitting here, Ms Riley,' Isla said. 'I'm in the way.' But even though she knew that she should move, she made no attempt to get up, only tucked her feet in towards her so that her knees were level with her collar, to make room for Ms Riley to get by.

'Nell is fine,' she said. 'Call me Nell.' Although she was much older than Isla – in her eighties at least – there was a liveliness radiating from her that Isla wasn't in possession of these days. 'I'm on my way to visit Oonagh Moody,' she announced, 'your neighbour.' As if Isla didn't know. When the weather was fine, Isla often saw Nell in the garden next door visiting Oonagh and Walter Moody, though Nell herself lived in the retirement home down the road. She used to slip Molly boiled sweets over the fence, sometimes dropping them in the flower bed to be found later if they weren't home.

'That's nice,' Isla said, and as an afterthought, 'Have a lovely time.'

Isla had expected Nell to go then, but instead she kept standing there, looking at her.

'Oonagh's not well,' Nell said.

'I'm sorry to hear that.'

'There's something going round, I think.' She licked spittle from her bottom lip. 'Why are you sat here like this?'

'I don't know,' Isla said. 'No real reason.'

Nell cocked her head, like a bird. 'You're upset.'

There was a mark of something on one of Isla's knees, soil maybe, crusted onto the fabric of her jeans, and she scraped at it with her fingernail, watched as it turned to chalky dust. She was suddenly exhausted; the afternoon had been draining on a deep level, and she wanted Nell to leave.

'Everyone's upset these days,' Nell continued.

'They're cutting down the woods,' Isla said. 'I think it's reasonable to be upset by that.'

Nell nodded. 'I've a bad feeling about them meddling with her like that.'

'Her?'

'Mother Nature; the woods.'

And because Isla said nothing in response, she added, 'And with a history like ours, too.'

Isla gazed up at her, shielding her eyes from the sunlight glaring off the ford.

'I suppose you don't know,' Nell said. 'I suppose you haven't heard about what happened here centuries ago.'

Isla shook her head. She was aware that the church and

the cottage on the river beside the stone bridge were all that remained of the original village, which everyone referred to as Old Hesket. But she'd not cared to find out what had happened to it, why it had disappeared in the first place.

'Oh, all kinds of strange things were happening back then, you see, things that people couldn't explain, that frightened them. Of course I can't know what came first, whether it was the curse that brought the witch trials to Hesket, or if the village was cursed after, *because* of them.'

Isla thought of the book she was editing, the one that Daniel was designing the cover for. It was an anthology of uncanny tales from Norfolk, and in it, there were anecdotes of haunted buildings and illicit burials, a monster that lurks in the rivers. She'd read aloud an earnest section of folklore to Geraldine only yesterday, concerning a supposed witch who was buried alive in the foundations of a church, and from her wooden leg a giant oak tree now stood in the nave of its ruins. *Oh, it's fun, isn't it*, Geraldine said, *that sort of stuff.*

'I didn't know there'd been witches in Hesket until I saw it in the petition.'

'Nine of them.' Nell nodded. 'All killed, of course, hanged from trees in those very woods over there, on the same ground the developers are wanting to interfere with. Quite brutal, actually, what was done to them, the torture they'd have suffered through. Can you imagine not being allowed to sleep for days on end, then being nearly drowned, and *then* hanged from your neck until you were dead, maybe even left up there until you rotted, and why? Because you made a comment that rubbed someone the wrong way.'

'That's awful,' Isla said, though she was aware Nell was talking *at* her, as if she were delivering a lecture, and that it probably didn't matter whether she responded or not.

'They wouldn't have even been buried in the churchyard after,' Nell was saying, 'which was a big deal back then, when religion was so much more important than it is now. I imagine those poor souls are still in Spry Wood, probably buried in the same place they fell after their bodies were finally cut down, in unhallowed ground, graves unmarked.' She sighed, ran her hand down the front of her coat, as if smoothing it. 'And then there came the flood, not long after. Sixteen forty-seven, I believe it was. Destroyed the village completely. I think it was a bit of poetic justice: they condemned those women in water and then the water got them back.' At the top of the road, the church bell began to ring out, the sound tinny and charming. 'Look it up if you don't believe me. The flood is public record. Hesket was a ghost for years after; wasn't resettled again until the eighteen hundreds, and it's much smaller, obviously, only this road.'

'Have there been many floods since?'

'Just the one, as far as I know.'

'And you think the developers should be told about it?' Isla said. 'Because maybe if there's a history of flooding in the area, they'll not want to build.'

'That's not what I'm concerned about,' Nell said. 'You've missed the point. I'm saying nothing good has ever come from opening old wounds. It's cursed ground, and they're going to traipse in and disturb it.'

'Oh, Ms Riley,' Isla protested, as politely as she could, 'don't be so silly.'

When Geraldine asked how Daniel was getting on with the commission, Isla lied and said that it was looking good, that she was excited to see where he went with it, even though he hadn't shown her anything. She could plot his activity through the posters that materialised like a network of fungi (which he'd once told her were more closely related to humans than plants) all over the neighbouring villages and hamlets, the nearest market town of Dereham, tracing how little time he'd spent working in the lean-to by the miles he'd covered.

One night, Daniel announced that he was meeting his friends, Liam and Darius, for drinks at a pub in Elsing. While he was out, Isla read for a while on the sofa, but soon felt restless and wandered to the kitchen, standing at the back door to get some fresh air. She heard whispers in the garden next door – Paul and his boys. After a few moments, there came the squeal of his gate, and she saw their shadowy figures appear beyond the hedge. She stood there, watching them walk out across the meadow by the light of a single torch until her skin pimpled from the chill, and she retreated again to the sofa to spend the rest of her evening half-watching whatever was on the television. Daniel came home only an hour later and sat on the coffee table in front of her, blocking the screen. He smelled sweet, like incense or oud perfume, instead of booze, and his cheeks and nose were blotched pink, as if he'd been crying. She put her hands on his legs, pressed gently. 'How're the lads?'

He burst into sniffling tears.

She put her arms around his waist, sitting close on the table beside him with her chin on his shoulder. It happened like this sometimes, one of them reduced, the other consoling.

'It was unreal, Isla. I wouldn't have believed it if I didn't see for myself.'

'What's that, then?' she said softly.

'I went to a medium,' he said. 'A clairvoyant.'

It was a strange thing to come out of his mouth. 'What do you mean? At the pub?'

'I don't know what I was expecting from it, but I just felt so ...' Tears were caught in his eyelashes. 'And the most amazing thing happened.' He began to smile, a smile so luminous it almost looked like laughter. 'She was there: Molly. I know it was her.'

It was difficult to take in just what he was saying. Her mind was still processing that he'd gone to a medium in the first place, and not the pub like he'd said he was. 'I don't understand. Where were Liam and Darius?'

He turned to her then, took her wrists in his hands. 'Listen,' he said, 'Molly's in Spry Wood.'

It stunned her, the way he said it, so simply and surely.

'Think about physics,' he continued excitedly, the words coming quick. 'There's a law of conservation that states energy can't be destroyed; it can only be transferred from one form to another. People – our matter, our atoms – are made of energy, aren't we? And after we die, the body redistributes that energy – it doesn't just cease to exist; it's transformed.

So just imagine if she's out there now, waiting to be identified in a new form. It's not beyond belief, is it? And you remember how connected she was to nature ...'

He was rambling, trying to convince her of this entirely bizarre idea. It occurred to her that she should march down to wherever he'd gone and tell that medium, whoever they were, that they ought to be more careful, that some people are too vulnerable, that it was taking advantage. But the more he went on, the more animated he grew, and the more she came to recognise that actually, he probably needed this. People had believed in intangibilities for thousands of years, and these things that were not visible and, likely, not real had somehow comforted, and she knew that was what this must be now, comfort-seeking, because the development had dredged things up, made things raw again.

'Isn't it amazing?' he said, his eyes shining.

There was undoubtedly a change in Daniel since his visit to the medium, a quiet energy that had been absent now returned. He was constantly in motion, introspective and occupied the way he used to be by a project, and shut himself in the lean-to for extended periods. He'd not brought up that strange night – his almost manic insistence they entertain the possibility of an afterlife – since it happened. Probably, he was embarrassed. It wasn't like him to get carried away by an idea so in opposition to logic; he was disparaging of the kinds of people who believed in conspiracies.

'How's it going in there?' she said, after a week of hardly seeing him.

'Good.' He sounded lighter than he had in months.

Emboldened, she said, 'Do you think it'll be ready in time?'

'What do you mean?'

'Do I need to ask for an extension?'

'Oh.' He paused. 'Yeah. Maybe.'

'Can I see it?'

He shook his head. 'You just need to give me some space to work.' He did not sound impatient; it was softer than that. 'I'm feeling more productive than I have in ages.' He kissed the top of her head, as if unconsciously, and the act surprised her; the spell of his melancholia had for so long disallowed affection. She was relieved mostly, and even though his improvement was down to a brief dalliance with something absurd and fanciful, at least his mood had shifted, at least he was working. She'd tell Geraldine he was making progress, ask about getting him more time.

When the news came that the village's petition had failed, she expected him to sob, fall to pieces, but he only drew her a bath of oils and salts, and then went out as usual. She waited on the edge of the steaming tub, poised to slip into the water in case he'd forgotten something and came home again; after long enough had passed that it would be unlikely he'd do so, she wrapped herself in her robe and went to Molly's room. She closed the door behind her, even though she was alone in the house, and looked at all the things that once had life but now just sat there. The ear of a stuffed rabbit still had that honeyed stink from being mouthed like a dummy. The soft helmet Molly decorated with a rainbow of stickers retained its shape on top of the low drawers, as if it had only just been taken off. *The Animals of Farthing Wood* that remained open on the little table by the window and childish illustrations of magpies stuck over every wall. The healthy move would've been to box most of it up for charity, keep the sentimental bits and jettison the rest. Isla knelt beside the bed, lifting the duvet just enough to slip her head beneath. And she stayed there with her chest on the mattress for just a little while, in the place where Molly used to lie.

They'd liked to walk, the three of them, out in nature and all Her sullen moods. The river walk was a favourite, out the back gate and across the hay meadow, through the woods following the water to the little bridge made of arched stone where they'd spot the silhouettes of darting fish, then back home by the village road. The pheasant walk was a bit shorter, wilder; the sugar beet walk took most of the day and was reserved for long weekends. The pig walk they did once and never again. Mostly, though, it was the woods. It had often taken an age no matter which they did, because Daniel and Molly kept halting to admire and identify and discuss, their way made up of erratic deviations and long, stagnant minutes spent peering beneath overgrown green and into hollows, the high canopies above. They wore tracks across the meadow through uneven lumps of tussock grass, stretches of woodland riddled with stones and roots and spider-legged twigs. Molly was prone to falling, sudden plunges that were difficult to predict. There was no identifiable cause for her condition, and it was refractory, meaning medication wasn't effective and their only options were either surgery – one to separate the two halves of her brain and then another, later, to remove an area of it entirely, which seemed too brutal for someone so small still – or the neurostimulator she'd had implanted beneath the skin on her chest, which would not rid her of the seizures entirely, but would help to control them. Outside, she wore the protective soft helmet because the drop seizures were particularly hard, sparked by patterns of sunlight flashing through the fretwork of treetops and the high heat of summer; one had split the back of her head when she was only four and from then on, they'd stuck to venturing out on overcast days. It was unlikely, they were told, that she'd even be able to drive without being triggered from the light flaring across the windshield on a bright day, but that had been a worry for the future, far from the girl who raced through the woods in search of bat hollows and fox dens in the drizzling rain.

'Watch your feet or you'll trip,' Isla warned. 'Dan, will you hold her at least?'

He might pick Molly up then, hitch her across his back as they ambled off, but inevitably she'd be let down again just as soon as something else required their attention, Isla's appeal forgotten. She didn't know when she'd agreed to let him be the fun parent.

She made herself useful by keeping an eye out for magpies, which were Molly's favourite because she believed they dropped gifts for her from the tree while she played below in the garden – bits of tinfoil, colourful little pebbles, snails, all landing by her feet. Not that Molly needed her help finding them. In her ladybird wellies and coat sleeves rolled at the wrist, she'd identify birdsong with all the seriousness and aplomb of Attenborough, her eyes squeezed shut, listening. Isla could pick out the truncated screech of a pheasant, like a rooster being strangled mid-crow, but all the small birds sounded indistinct to her.

'Blackbird,' Molly said, pleased with herself. 'Chaffinch.'

Daniel, having been her tutor, delighted in her answers.

It was not that she was jealous; it was not that at all. Her own dad had been more interested in his cars than her, and she was thrilled, relieved, that history had not repeated itself. She knew that she should tell them to go out alone, that it would be nice for just the two of them without her loitering, pre-emptively stoppering their fun or trying not to look at the phone she clutched in her jacket pocket when they spoke of things foreign to her, words like *siskin* and *pipistrelle, lesser celandine*, but always, always, she never could.

Daniel started going on walks without Isla, leaving without a word so that she didn't know when precisely he'd gone, or else he was already out by the time she got home from work. She'd see him from the window returning with something found: a leaf or flower that he'd shut himself away with in the lean-to.

There were clothes, more than usual, discarded throughout the house, perfumed with earth and sweat, and once, she was sure, something musky, feral, like an animal. Increasingly, Daniel was home long enough to wash and eat, to lock himself in the lean-to until nightfall and then head out again, often until long after she'd gone to bed. He began to sleep in Molly's room so as not to disturb Isla, but she lay awake anyway, batting away her concerns at his behaviour, justifying these new night-time wanderings as another part of his process. She imagined the kinds of specimens he was trying to source for the cover design, the photographs he was taking to work from; he told her long ago that most wildlife was nocturnal. In the morning, she'd find he'd left the back door wide open, the kitchen littered with bits blown in overnight and the tiles icy beneath her socks. A crisp, curled leaf might splinter underfoot so that she had to pick the pieces of it from her sole and flick them out the door before locking it shut. He'd claim that the mechanism must be faulty, or that he'd been too tired coming in late last night to remember to close it behind him. *You're letting out all the heat*, she'd scold. *Anything could come in.*

There'd been a fox once. How it got in, she wasn't sure, but there it was when she walked into the kitchen to sweep the floor. Molly was giggling as its long pink tongue lapped butter greedily from her outstretched hand, its glistening canines and hungry eyes, how near it was to her daughter, how easily her small fingers could have been lost to its mouth. It was the precariousness of the situation that alarmed Isla, if in that moment there'd been a sudden burst of activity in Molly's brain, like an electrical storm in her head, that sent her defencelessly to the floor, and if Isla hadn't walked in when she did ... Its claws skittered on the tiles as she swung the broom and shooed it out, and Molly, amber eyes furious, being the one to chastise *her*, the backwardness of it. *Why did you do that?* she wailed. *What if she doesn't come back?*

Daniel's posters had been up for the better part of September when Isla knocked on the lean-to door and waited; inside, the lamps were all on and she could see him moving beyond the warped glass. The garden was unruly after a long summer left to itself, at once stunted by drought and overrun with hardy green weeds, so that it was caught between various phases of life and death. By the door, at her feet, were piles of things discarded: clumps of uprooted bracken, lichen-covered sticks, a branch riddled with black tails of fungi, something else small and brown, and unidentifiable with decay. When he finally unlocked the door, he opened it only a few inches, and blocked her view inside with his body.

'What's this mess?' she said.

He hesitated before answering. 'It's what I'm working on.'

'Oh?'

'They're all the wrong thing,' he said. 'None of them feel right yet.' She knew that he had to be inspired by something to be able to fully capture it in a drawing, and it wasn't unreasonable that it was taking time to get back into things, after having not worked properly in so long.

'What is it that's smelling?' She grimaced, nudged at some bracken with her toe. 'You've not got animals in here, have you?'

He made an irascible noise. 'I'm a bit busy, Isla.'

'I spoke to Geraldine about the extension.' She eyed the pile a moment longer, and then turned her attention to him.

'She was a bit reluctant, to be honest. There's a hard deadline for the printing company; you can have an extra fortnight, no more.'

'Right.' He sighed. 'I don't know if that's going to work.'

'It needs to.'

He drummed on the doorframe with his fingers.

'If you're stuck, I could take a look.' She moved towards him.

'No,' he said. 'It's not that. It's just time.'

'She doesn't want to have to find someone else.'

'I'll get it done.' He rubbed the spot between his eyebrows. 'I will.'

'You have to. The book will be delayed otherwise, and you agreed to payment on delivery.'

He seemed to take notice of her then, as if seeing her properly, before reaching out to stroke her cheek, his touch tender. 'I know how shit I've been,' he said quietly. 'I know we need the money.'

She leaned into his hand, pressed her mouth to his wrist.

'I've been absent,' he admitted. 'I don't want to let you down. That's not my intention.'

'Then don't.'

He gazed past her, towards the woods, and she thought how sad he looked then, how confined in his solitude.

'Come in the house,' she said. 'Spend some time with me.'

He rested his temple against the door, considering her invitation. 'All right,' he said finally. 'One sec.' He retreated into the lean-to, closing the door firmly after him, so that she was stood out in the dusk; when he'd turned off all the lights and opened it again, she couldn't make out anything inside before he locked it behind him.

'You've become very secretive,' she said.

'I've always been like that.'

'No,' she said. 'Only lately.'

'I have a request.' She saw then that he held a small bowl. 'Blackberries. Can you please bake a crumble? I'd do it, but it'll turn out all gluey or something.' He'd once made a cake for her birthday, and presented it to her with burnt edges and a raw, liquidy middle. 'I picked them today,' he said. 'From the usual spot.'

It had been a long time since she'd baked anything. Inside, beneath the bright kitchen light, she took the bowl from him and inspected the berries. 'Most of these aren't ripe enough. It'll be too tart.'

'That's all right,' he said cheerfully. 'We're sweet enough already.' And then made one of those *ba-dum-tss* noises.

Isla pulled a face. 'It'd taste better if we waited.'

'Please.'

'Why?'

'Because I miss blackberry crumble.'

She knew then what this was about. In autumn the blackberries grew in Spry Wood in large cascading thickets, and it had been one of Molly's favourite things to do, to go out and fill old takeaway containers and sauce jars with fruit to cart home for baking. They grew so plentifully that the three of them had often gone every weekend and returned with a bounty to make a tip of the kitchen; even Molly had come to know the recipe by heart. And because

Isla desperately missed blackberry crumble too, she rinsed them in the sink.

She tossed the berries with sugar and then tipped them into a pie dish. The topping was made by rubbing together butter and flour in a bowl with her fingers, before stirring in more sugar, and then she spooned the mixture on top of the fruit in shapes, because that was what Molly used to do – clouds and flowers and rabbits with long ears.

It was, admittedly, not her best attempt. The filling was too sharp; the topping pale and doughy. Neither could have more than a small piece. 'I'm out of practice,' she apologised.

'I think it's wonderful.' There were small crumbs caught in his stubble. He stopped her from scraping the rest into the compost bin and tucked it onto a shelf in the fridge.

He called her at Geraldine's house the next day, sounding out of breath, incensed. 'There's people in hi-vis, ripping out bloody trees.'

'Already?' Her mind flashed briefly to Nell and the things she'd said, but just as quickly, the thought went from her.

'Did you know they were going to come this soon?'

The question, his accusatory tone, annoyed her. 'How would I? I know as much as you do.' She could hear birds twittering; he was outside. 'Don't walk over there.'

He must have sighed then, because the line crackled loudly. 'I need to get going,' he said, and hung up.

At home later she went out to check on him, worried that the start of the woodland cull might have reignited his despair, but the lean-to was dark.

It was a lovely evening to be outside. Ribbons of electric orange and pink crossed the sky, and she went to the back gate to gaze out over the meadow and catch the last moments of sunset. In the distance, she saw Daniel walking to the woods and went after him. Ahead, the treeline was silhouetted against the sky, an opaque boundary between a wild world and their own, and he was soon lost to its shadow. A bat swooped just in front of her head, angular and skittish, and she faltered, repelled. The light was quickly disappearing. She'd not find him in the dark.

On the walk back to the house she needed her phone torch to navigate the meadow, filled as it was with ankle-twisting burrows and grassy mounds. She might not have seen it had the light not glared on the white enamel: tucked beneath the meadow-side of their hedge was the pie dish, empty except for hardened globs of blackberry where it had smeared across the surface, Veinous Blood Red. There were marks in the filling, like a scrape of teeth, the rest of it licked clean.

She decided that she would make another crumble, a better crumble, one that was properly cooked and sweet so that he didn't leave it out for the animals. She would deliver it to the door of the lean-to, and maybe she would tell him its colours, and maybe, in return, he would let her in.

At the edge of the woods, she could see where the clearing of vegetation had begun ahead of the development; there was a large pile of brushwood and scrub, branches laden with crab apple among them, and left in their place were sockets of loose, empty earth. It looked unnaturally barren, like a baseball pitch, among all this wild. Because it was the weekend, there was no one there to turn her away, to see her quickly fill her pockets with firm round fruit; it was too much a waste to leave the apples behind to rot when they were perfectly good and alive.

The sight too awful to linger any longer, she took the path through a tunnel of trees to where the blackberries grew, and realised how transformed it all was after having not been here for a while, unrecognisable from the woods where she'd gone walking so many times in the past, as if all the trees had got up and planted themselves in a new configuration. Or was it that it felt somehow denser now, despite the unseasonal thinning of leaves, the gnarled branches seemingly lower and claustrophobic in a way they hadn't been before, that made her uneasy? And there was the quiet – the woods she knew had been full of birdsong and the scurrying of squirrels, of small animals nosing in the undergrowth. Now there was only the wind through brittle leaves and the creaking of timber, as if the trees themselves were stirring awake after a long sleep. And there was a weight to the place now, a foreboding. Probably it was all in her head, disquiet bubbling to the surface because she knew that in the coming days it would all be gone, wouldn't it, the trees plucked out like feathers from skin, and it was this that cast a frightful gloom which settled into every inch of bark, every fallen leaf.

A few days had done the final flush of blackberries good, though they were not as abundant this year, not without rain. Many of them still had the ruby colouring of wine, but some were soft and darkly plump, and inked her fingers when she pulled them free of the brambles. The air smelled pleasantly smoky, like someone had lit a stove fire (but strangely not yet of autumn, of damp loam and sweetly rotting leaves, the drought having suspended the breaking down of leaf litter, so that it crackled drily on the ground's surface). To come out on her own had often felt too vulnerable a thing to do before, but the fresh air was invigoratingly sharp in her lungs, and it began to dispel the feeling she'd held in the whole of her for such a long time, like a swallowed and stagnating howl.

She prolonged the walk back with a pilgrimage to the past, and visited the Grandmother Oak, so named by Molly for how old and great it was. She found again the pond, the small clearing, but the hawthorn that Molly used to pretend was her castle wasn't where Isla remembered it stood. She left the path in search of it, picking her way through the wilder parts of the undergrowth, skeletal branches hooking her clothes. When she uncovered it, half-hidden behind some overgrown holly, it was heavy with red haw berries, and at its base, strangely, was a cage trap, large enough for a fox. And there, at the back where the bait should go, was a padded soft helmet covered in stickers as iridescent as fish scales. She stared at it, recognising each carefully applied shape: a scattering of small colourful hearts, a blue dinosaur and a cartoon mouse, a scratch-and-sniff strawberry ice-cream cone.

Bewildered then, like a fly hitting glass.

She couldn't make sense of just what it was she saw, knew only that she felt an intense betrayal – its exact cause and contours obscured by shock – and that Molly's helmet did not belong there, in the dark and lonely wood.

Seizing the cage, she shook it, wrestling with the spring-loaded door until the helmet was out, and then threw the trap as hard as she could, only for it to land unsatisfyingly on the spiny branches of the hawthorn and hang there, askew, just above the ground. She tucked the helmet into her jacket and wondered, horrified, outraged, at how many other parts of Molly he might have scattered – and for what?

Anger propelled her home, and she shouted his name as she charged through the garden gate, and at the lean-to door. She rattled the handle, yanked and kicked at it, before bashing it with a rock until the door whined open. The light inside was dim, the room musty and still. It looked so different than it had the last time she'd been in, no longer neatly organised, but a shambles. There were papers strewn all over – on the walls, the floor, every surface – what appeared to be lists, and various hand-drawn maps of Spry Wood. There were things he'd collected, bits of bark and bones and feathers, the rotting, stinking body of a toad, the tiny curled foot of a bird, and pinned to a cork board were wilted flowers and pillows of moss, tufts of fur in browns and reds. And everywhere, there were his paintings, less considered than she was used to seeing from him, more frenzied and abstract, half-finished, collaged over every wall. She approached one, a rendering of a barn owl, and there, written beneath in Daniel's hand, *eyes – lightest brown wing feathers*. A large X had been slashed over the owl, and all around were more crossed out images: *fur of a weasel; the cap of a birch polypore fungi; the shell of a mature acorn.* There were dozens and dozens in various hues of brown, and as she followed them around the room she read each aloud like an incantation, searching for some vestige of meaning, some way in which they could possibly be the commission for Geraldine, until she reached one of the largest paintings, a hare that stared back at her, and there, circled again and again, its distinctively amber eye, *the irises of a hare*, and she understood with such a swift and undeniable clarity that it wasn't inspiration for the cover design he'd been hunting for, but Molly, that the crumble, the helmet, had both been used to try to lure her home because he'd believed a ridiculous story from some psychic, some fraud, about her not really being gone, even though she was – she was – and all that time he'd spent in the woods without Isla, all those selfish hours searching and collecting and categorising, it was all prioritising a fantasy over what she needed from him, after she'd been so tolerant, so patient of his behaviour, his unstable moods, his willingness to let her shoulder the burden of keeping them going, and in return he'd done nothing but waste weeks constructing his own self-serving nomenclature of their daughter, all for the futile and absurd pursuit of trying to find Molly, who was not in the woods, before it was felled. It was a transgression, and it had forced her to transgress, too, in lying about his progress on the commission, and now she'd have to come clean to Geraldine.

The picture of the hare tore as she pulled it from the wall.

She gathered as many as she could hold and carried them into the kitchen, shaking, as she searched the drawers for a lighter. Sparking it, she held the flame to each painting over the sink, held it so hard that her thumb stung where it pressed into the flint wheel, and she watched as they caught and burned into nothingness. And just as she ran the tap to start flushing the ash away, Daniel appeared at the back door wearing only a T-shirt. He was holding a young hare in his arms, a leveret, wrapped in his jumper, and was incandescently cooing at its oversized and clumsy ears, its thickly velveteen fur, and she could smell the warmness of it as he approached, sweet and delicate like hay, and it was darling like her and had the honey-puddled eyes of her, but it was still just a wild thing.

Rio

The room was dark but for the moonlight on the floor by the window, and the pillar candles and tealights arranged in the centre of the circular table. It was a small room, one of two downstairs, and filled with ornate heavy furniture that gave the space a morose, oppressive quality. Its sombre appearance, at least, must have made it easier to create the right atmosphere on nights that Madam Celia conjured the dead.

She did this for a living, the conjuring, or so she claimed.

Which is why Rio was sat in an old armchair in the gloom, about to observe a séance. This was their second meeting; yesterday, Madam Celia had given her a palm reading.

'I'll have to use my phone as a light so I can see when I jot things down,' Rio said. 'I hope that's okay.'

A brief silence, and then Madam Celia cleared her throat. 'I thought you were recording?' Candlelight emphasised the way her make-up made her ageing skin look like crêpe paper. Perhaps in an effort to appear younger, she'd applied the foundation thickly, with bright pink whirls of blush like a marionette. Her frizzy hair had been dyed a lurid orange, and an unflattering shade of taupe lipstick bled into the lines around her mouth.

'I am.' Rio held up the phone perched beside her on the chair. 'The notebook is for nuances.'

'Ah.' Madam Celia sounded approving. 'My work is all about nuance.'

Rio could understand the allure of this kind of thing, the prospect of the supernatural, the spectacle of the occult; there was a reason why Victorian parlour games had been so popular.

'What normally happens during a séance?' It was a probing question; she already knew, of course, had seen enough movies to know what to expect.

'Oh,' Madam Celia said casually, 'communing with the dead, maybe a spot of levitation.'

Rio's instinct was to laugh.

'No,' Madam Celia said, whimsically. 'That wasn't a joke.'

She held a stick of incense over a candle to catch, then began wafting it around the room.

Rio noted down the wafting.

Madam Celia must have been keeping an eye on her, because she explained, 'I'm just setting the scene, so to speak. My mother, rest her soul, always said it's all in the details, anyone good at their craft knows that.'

'Was your mother a clairvoyant, too?'

'A stage actress. She was a wondrous Miranda in *The Tempest* at the Maddermarket Theatre in Norwich.' She closed her eyes and inhaled deeply through her nose.

'What did she think of this?'

Madam Celia exhaled loudly – 'Of what?' – and then inhaled a second time.

'What you do.'

Her eyes fluttered open, and she gazed coyly at Rio before speaking. 'Why, she was disappointed that I didn't follow in her footsteps and become an actress.' And then she waved the incense around her head, a dozen or so silver bangles clattering softly on her wrist as she hummed something sprightly but unidentifiable.

Rio made a note: *Eccentricity = performance?* 'Have you done any acting?'

Madam Celia stood the incense in a small cup, pride evident in her voice as she said, 'I was raised in the theatre.'

When Rio arrived earlier, Madam Celia had launched into a monologue about her life as a soothsayer, which was, she said, what people with her proclivities were called back in the day; like Mother Shipton, only with less barren cave, and more bulky walnut-stained furniture that cramped the room.

Madam Celia draped a purple shawl across her shoulders, and Rio noticed her tucking the Primark label out of view.

'Have you ever worked with actors?' Rio said.

'In what sense?'

Rio considered how best to ask without offending her. 'Like for effect, maybe.'

'Is that what you think I'd do?'

They regarded each other in silence. Rio was used to people being evasive. It was something she encountered all the time in her line of work, but also at the poker games she frequented at the Lucky Fortune Casino in the city. Poker was a game of non-disclosure. She had to pay attention to fleeting changes in body language, to minute fluctuations of facial expression, and as a result, she'd learned to read people quite well, or so she'd thought; she'd been in a losing pit for some time now, even though she was doing everything right, and she was impatient for the cards to turn in her favour again.

It struck her that sitting around a séance table would be not unlike sitting round a poker table: the same exhilaration of the unknown; the thrilling possibility of what could happen; the fantasy of leaving with everything you'd hoped for.

Rio wrote, *Madam Celia keeps her cards close.*

There was a soft knock at the door, followed swiftly by the dull rapping of Madam Celia's shoes as she hurried past Rio and out of the room. Rio leaned forward so that she could see the narrow kitchen, faintly illuminated by the streetlamp outside. The shadowy figure of Madam Celia stood a few moments with her hand on the doorknob, perhaps to elicit suspense. When she swept it open, she did so with a flourish, startling the curly-haired woman wearing glasses on the other side. The woman, who looked to be in her early twenties – ten or so years younger than Rio – smiled nervously. 'Hello. I'm here for . . .' She squinted past Madam Celia and into the dark of the house. 'Are you Madam Celia?'

'What's your name, luv?'

'Oh.' The woman touched her glasses. 'Fiona?'

Fiona was one of three due tonight. Rio had seen the

names scrawled beneath a shopping list when she arrived: *loo roll, eggs, stilton, fabric softener, Daniel, Fiona, G. Alexander.* Which made five of them for the evening; like the five cards in a hand.

'This way, please.' Madam Celia walked – glided – back into the room so quietly that Rio wondered if she'd removed her shoes. 'Don't mind the journalist in the corner.'

Rio waved.

'A journalist?' Fiona said excitedly. 'How fun.'

Madam Celia had assured Rio that the participants this evening had agreed to her sitting in on their session.

'Oh, it's not a big deal, really.' Madam Celia's voice dripped with faux modesty. 'Just a human-interest story, isn't that right?'

Actually, it was the 'East Anglian Eccentrics' column that had been running longer than Rio had been alive, and highlighted unusual people in different parts of Norfolk, Suffolk, Cambridgeshire and Essex; this week, her options had been either Madam Celia or a man who claimed to commune telepathically with crabs in Cromer, but Rio didn't need to reveal that.

'Really?' Fiona sounded impressed. 'Like Louis Theroux?'

'It's for the *Norfolk Times*,' Rio said.

Fiona frowned sympathetically. 'I'm sorry.' And then, as if in compensation, 'You can put me in it if you want. I consent.'

Rio took down her details.

'I can sense that she's a little sceptical of my abilities,' Madam Celia told Fiona. 'As all journalists are, of course. But she'll believe by tonight's end.' And then she threw the curtains open wider, flinging them dramatically to reveal that the house was nestled in the crook of an old churchyard with crumbling, lichen-covered gravestones visible from the window, jutting at odd angles like crooked teeth, and beyond them, an ink-dark sky and spectral clouds, the emptiness of an open meadow washed by the full moon.

'Wow,' Fiona said appreciatively.

'I've seen will-o'-the-wisps in that meadow from this very window,' Madam Celia said, as if to impress them further. 'On nights the moon is like this one.'

Four knocks at the front door, and Madam Celia left them standing at the window. Rio thought of all those people that had been entombed beneath the gravestones for an eternity and were now just skeletons, long forgotten by anyone living, judging by the state of them. The graveyard would probably be the most authentic part of the evening.

'Do you think they're real?' Fiona said.

'Please do come inside.' Madam Celia's voice floated in from the kitchen. 'You said your name was Daniel?'

'So,' Rio said, 'how did you find out about Madam Celia?'

'Instagram,' Fiona said. 'You?'

'Google. Do you mind if I ask what made you sign up for a group session? I'd have thought most people would want their experience to be a bit more private, considering.'

'To be honest,' Fiona lowered her voice, 'I thought about a one-on-one, but her rates are kind of extortionate.'

'Of course,' Madam Celia was saying, as she entered the room, 'I saw you putting up those posters last week.' She gestured vaguely in the direction of the road.

'Yeah.' The man called Daniel had muddy troughs beneath his eyes, as if he'd not slept in a long time, and a dark wash of stubble. 'The development. It's outrageous.'

Madam Celia nodded politely, made agreeable noises as he talked animatedly about the proposed plan and its devastating impact on the natural landscape. Fiona watched them from the window, her posture expectant, as if waiting for an introduction. Daniel was still talking as he pulled out a chair and sat at the table. 'But mostly,' he said, 'what kind of person wants to get behind the destruction of the environment, you know? What kind of monster?'

'You feel quite passionately about it,' Madam Celia said. 'I can sense that you're a very passionate person.'

'Yeah, well, my daughter was—' He sighed wearily then, as if he didn't have the energy to continue whatever he'd been about to say.

'Mmm?' Madam Celia pressed.

He'd just given her something she could use.

'It's a really special place to us, that's all.'

Rio knew all about tells from the nights spent at poker, had come to learn how some of the other players gave themselves away; one of the regulars, Simon, would adjust his position if he had a good hand, shifting forward ever so slightly in his seat, as if in preparation to lay his cards triumphantly on the table.

'They're doing that sort of thing in Honingham, too.' Fiona sat in the chair beside Daniel. 'There's a motorway or something? I don't know.'

'That's the Western Link.' Daniel removed his coat and

hung it over his chair. 'Also known as the Wensum Link because it'll cut through the Wensum Valley.'

Fiona did the same, and Rio guessed what Madam Celia was probably thinking: susceptible to influence, this one. 'I suppose it'll relieve congestion? That it'll boost tourism? That's what they've said.'

Daniel was shaking his head. 'Don't believe what they tell you.' He checked off his fingers: 'Killing irreplaceable thousand-year-old trees, rising costs, increased carbon emissions. Their campaign is a scam.'

'Oh,' Fiona said. 'Shouldn't the government stop it, then? Labour are all about protecting nature.'

'That's what they said *before* the election. Now they're going to build a million homes on greenbelt sites. We can't rely on them; it's up to us, the people, to save the environment.' He leaned towards Fiona, quite intently, and said, 'I hope you're protesting.'

Fiona glanced over at Rio and then again at Daniel.

'Write a letter to your MP,' he implored. 'Rally your neighbours. Do whatever you have to do, but don't do nothing. This is *actually* important.'

Fiona looked a bit stunned. 'Definitely.' She nodded slowly. 'I will.' And then, perhaps to deflect his attention, she gestured to Rio. 'She's a journalist.'

'A journalist?' He turned to Madam Celia, scandalised. 'Why is there a journalist here?'

'Did I not warn you beforehand?' Madam Celia said innocently.

'I'm not here to be fodder for a bloody tabloid.'

'If I could,' Rio said. 'I assure you that I won't use any material without permission; in fact, I'll omit you entirely if you prefer. The article won't focus on any of you.'

'She's writing a profile on Madam Celia,' Fiona said.

'A profile?' He looked at Rio, baffled. 'If you're after a story, why don't you investigate the development?'

Rio was embarrassed then; it was true the eccentrics column was not the worthiest of work. Perhaps she should transform this particular assignment, a fluff piece, into something more compelling, take the chance to unpick the magic trick and expose the ruse, and use it as leverage to get higher calibre assignments in the future.

Madam Celia was suddenly at Rio's side, squeezing her shoulder as she said, 'Would anyone like some tea?'

Rio covered her notebook with her hands. 'Yes, thanks.'

'This way then,' she said in a sing-song voice, and swept out of the room before the others had even finished politely declining.

Rio followed, grateful to remove herself from Daniel's disapproving glower.

In the dark of the kitchen, Madam Celia pulled Rio close, the whites of her eyes gleaming. 'Apologies for the confrontation just now,' she whispered. 'I assumed no one would mind. A misjudgement on my part.'

'You said you'd told them.'

'Well.' She cleared her throat softly. 'In the interest of full disclosure, I want you to know that I recognise that man. Daniel. I'm aware of who he is, I mean.' Madam Celia smelled faintly of lavender soap and stale coffee. 'He's my neighbour,' she continued. 'At least, he lives in the neighbourhood, a few houses down; not that I see him regularly. But I wanted to let you know, so you don't think I'm a phoney. I read his palm at the spring fête last year, and I'm sorry to say I sense that's why he's come now; I knew it as soon as I saw him.'

'And why's that?'

'Her presence is so strong in the room already.'

'Whose?'

'Ah.' Madam Celia held up her finger. 'I don't know her name yet. I don't know any details at all, only that there's a female spirit attached to him. Beyond that, I haven't yet tapped into. That's what the session is for.'

'He said he had a daughter,' Rio pointed out. 'Past tense.'

'And you think I'm making assumptions, picking up on clues to use to my advantage.'

Rio tried to be diplomatic. 'Maybe subconsciously.'

Madam Celia began pulling an assortment of drinkware out of the cupboard, including a bejewelled gin goblet and a large mug shaped like a cauldron that said *witches brew* in glow-in-the-dark writing.

'What did you predict for him at the spring fête?' Rio asked.

'Read,' Madam Celia corrected. 'I *read* hands. And actually,' she said sadly, 'it was the same thing I intuited for you.' She patted Rio's arm. 'What a coincidence.'

When Madam Celia had given Rio a reading yesterday, she'd scanned her palm the way someone would a menu.

'Hmm,' Madam Celia muttered to herself. 'Hmmm.'

'Anything interesting in my future?'

'Your life line is pretty good.' She pointed to the line rounding Rio's thumb. 'Clear and unbroken, which means a long and healthy life. Breaks on the fate line, which is this long one running from your middle finger to your wrist, indicates important changes will occur. And there, bridging the head and heart lines ...' She traced the small curve with her finger. 'A loss.'

'Loss?' She'd planned on going to the casino again after the séance was over. 'What sort of loss?'

'It doesn't give specifics.' She shrugged. 'A loss. But you've a triangle on Mercury, look.' She pointed to the lines etched below Rio's little finger. 'Success in your career.'

A classic shit sandwich, Rio thought. She was determined that she would not lose any more of her money. Her run of bad luck had been nothing short of uncanny: she'd played textbook games, yet consistently the most unlikely cards would come up and beat her hand, which was entirely maddening. Her frustration had made her rash and take chances she shouldn't have, and this had only made her lose more money. It was shocking how quickly the debt had racked up; she was now in it for thousands, all on her credit cards, and how could she possibly pay it off on her kind of wage? Yet she couldn't stop herself going, compelled to return time and again to take her chances, in the hope that she could possibly win and get herself out of the mess she was in. Thinking about it gave Rio a horrible sensation in her stomach, as if it were coiling in on itself as tightly as a snail's shell. 'How accurate is palmistry?'

Madam Celia smiled. 'Worried about your fate?'

Rio withdrew her hand. 'I saw a church next door. Interesting choice of location for someone in your profession.'

'The church people own this house. I think the vicar has taken it upon herself to keep an eye on me, make sure I'm not doing anything unsanctimonious.' The thought of this appeared to offend her. 'I suppose that I can't complain, though; rent's quite cheap.'

'She doesn't use your services, then?'

'I doubt she even approves,' Madam Celia said. 'Which is rich, because her job is just a dressed-up version of mine, as far as I'm concerned.'

'How so?'

'We both provide comfort.'

Rio thought about this. 'But aren't ghosts typically frightening?'

'Comfort and fear can go hand in hand. Surely, the presence of spirits also means there's the possibility that you and I can return after we die, and isn't that both a reassuring and an unnerving prospect? The idea that death *isn't* the end is in religion as much as it's in ghost stories.'

'That's quite insightful.' Rio checked her phone to make sure it was recording. 'Where is it you learned to do this kind of thing?'

Madam Celia gave Rio an assessing glance, as if deciding whether to divulge her hand so early in the game. 'Palmistry I learned; the rest is a gift I was born with.'

*

In the darkened kitchen, Madam Celia turned to peer at the illuminated oven clock. 'We're just waiting for one more before we can begin.'

And then, as if she'd summoned it herself, another knocking, sure and loud.

'Speak of the devil,' Rio said.

'Ah.' Madam Celia wagged her finger playfully. 'It's speak of the *spirits* in this house.' She hurried to the door, and when she opened it the streetlamp outside shone in like a spotlight. On the step stood a man in a bowler hat and jeans, with a carefully groomed Dali-esque moustache and a protruding stomach wrapped in a shiny maroon waistcoat; the effect was similar to fancy dress, like a half-arsed Dr Watson costume. He appeared to be waiting for Madam Celia to speak first, raising his eyebrows quizzically at her, as though she'd been the one to knock on *his* door. 'Mr Alexander, I presume?'

'Indeed that's me.' He said this with a sort of curtsey as he doffed his hat, the light gleaming on his bald head. 'G. Alexander.' He emphasised the initial, like he wanted her to enquire further.

Madam Celia obliged, perhaps to move things along. 'G?'

He placed his hat back on his head. 'Correct.' Then he smiled at her, lips closed and tightly narrow, as if he were holding in a mouthful of water, and didn't elaborate.

His amusement struck Rio as arrogant, and Madam Celia must have thought so too, because she didn't usher him inside like she had the others. Rather, she seemed suddenly apprehensive. 'Tell me, Mr Alexander, have you ever done anything like this before?'

'Once or twice.' He winked at her, drumming his fingers on his waistcoat.

For a long moment, Rio wasn't sure that he'd even be let in, wondered if the two of them would just go on observing one another on the threshold like that, but finally, Madam Celia stood aside and said coolly, 'The others are in the back room.'

'Then I suppose I'd better join them.' He strode past her as if he'd been there before, confident – no, cocky, the same way Rio felt if she managed to bluff her hand and make someone fold.

When Madam Celia shut the door, the swing of her arm was forceful enough to create a kind of vacuum, wafting Rio's hair.

'Ooh, look,' Fiona exclaimed from the other room. 'One of the candles has just gone out by itself. That's so spooky.'

The kitchen was dark again. 'Please go ahead,' Madam Celia said from the shadows as she fixed her shawl. 'I'll bring your drink through in a minute. Is nettle tea okay?'

Rio returned to the armchair in the corner of the room. The others were all sat round the table, bathed in a soft candlelight that rendered the contours of their faces in ghoulish shadows. Daniel was still talking about the development, his voice hushed now, punctuated by long silences that Fiona appeared to have given up trying to fill, while G. Alexander sat quietly scrutinising the room.

When Madam Celia returned, she placed the witch's cauldron by Rio's feet as Fiona eagerly pointed out the extinguished candle to her.

'Mmm.' Madam Celia nodded. 'The spirits are announcing their presence.'

Madam Celia has perfected the art of a knowing look.

'We can interpret that as our cue to begin.' She took the seat nearest the window, the churchyard silhouetted behind her a suitably dramatic backdrop. 'Our connecting with the spirits depends on each of us being open to receive anything that might occur this evening.'

G. Alexander smirked at the gravestones etched against the semi-darkened sky as if they were tacky Halloween decorations.

'*Disbelievers*,' Madam Celia said, gazing quite pointedly at everyone but G. Alexander, 'weaken the energy that's required of the session, making it much more difficult for the spirits to come through. It's imperative that everyone be open to whatever happens here tonight.' She straightened in her seat, an air of poise about her. 'Now, palms flat on the table, eyes closed, all of you, and breathing deeply.' She inhaled theatrically through her nose again.

The incense Madam Celia lit earlier was still heady in the room, and it lingered at the back of Rio's throat.

'I want you all to quiet your minds and concentrate your energy.'

They sat in silence this way for a few minutes; occasionally Madam Celia made a noise – a sigh or an *mmm* – as if tasting the room for otherworldly sensations. 'Can you feel that? The shift that's occurred?'

Fiona nodded.

The room was unchanged to Rio. She had a sip of nettle tea; it was bitter like spinach and tasted the way hay smelled.

'The spirits are ready,' Madam Celia announced solemnly. 'You may open your eyes.'

Fiona peered over her shoulder looking vaguely alarmed, as if she were expecting to be confronted with ghosts floating leisurely behind her. Even Daniel glanced quickly around the room; G. Alexander, however, was focused solely on Madam Celia, his face expressionless.

'Oh!' Madam Celia held up her palm with the kind of dramatic flair that looked as if it had been honed in front of a mirror. 'There's someone here who wants to make themselves known.' She pressed a finger to her temple as if in concentration. 'Go on,' she said to the room at large. 'They're very quiet, it's difficult to ... Yes, that's right. Come closer, my dear.' She paused for effect. 'I'm getting an M-something.'

Daniel's chair creaked as he leaned forward, captivated, eager.

'Marcus?' Fiona said then. 'Is it Marcus?'

A flicker of something in Madam Celia's face, before she nodded. 'I feel a tragedy connected to him? There's a sadness?'

Daniel sank back in his seat. He seemed suddenly restless, and scratched absently at the stubble on his cheeks, the sound like Velcro.

'He was involved in an accident and no one survived. It's been so difficult for my family. My aunt—'

'Please, only "yes" or "no" answers,' Madam Celia said. 'The death, it was very shocking.'

Rio thought this was a likely bet.

'Yes,' Fiona said.

'His presence is quite strong now; it's becoming more powerful.'

And then, a loud bang, like a heavy book being thrown to the floor, and the room was suddenly tense with frightful excitement, everyone wide-eyed and staring, surveying the room. Rio could not be certain where the sound had come from; she considered the possibility there might be someone hiding upstairs. 'Can Marcus do that again?' Rio said.

'Can you do that again?' Madam Celia asked the room.

Silence.

For a few moments there was nothing, and then a strange buzzing, like a vibration.

'Oh my God!' Fiona shrieked. 'The table!'

The table was rattling. Madam Celia threw her head back. 'Yes,' she exclaimed, 'we're listening.'

Daniel turned to Rio, wild-eyed. 'Are you seeing this?'

From the armchair, she had a view beneath the table if she slouched, and she shone the light of her phone towards it, hoping to reveal the subterfuge. But Madam Celia's legs were not touching it, not even close; it simply appeared to be a table, moving by itself.

The possibility that she should witness something incredible and unexplainable tonight had been preposterous to Rio. But watching the spectacle occur, she could not help but believe that it was real; it was happening, after all, in front of her eyes, and she could not deny that. It *was* unexplained. It *was* incredible.

Adrenalin lurched through her, the sensation unpleasant and transportive, so that it was as though she were leaving the casino again, overwhelmed at having lost, at her debt swelling even further beyond control.

The table stilled abruptly. Madam Celia began to nod, as if listening to a disembodied voice.

'He wants you to know that the presence you feel sometimes is him.'

'Yes.' Fiona smiled, overjoyed. 'I knew it was.'

'He cares very deeply for you. You had a bond.'

'Yes.'

'He says he's watching over you.'

Fiona sniffed. There were tears in her eyes.

'He wants you to tell your aunt that he's watching over her, too.'

Fiona's expression changed then. 'My aunt? That doesn't...' She shook her head. 'But she was driving the car. She died with him.'

G. Alexander appeared positively delighted.

Despite the error, Madam Celia did not falter. 'A miscommunication. My ability as a conduit is only as strong as the energy in the room. If everyone could please concentrate.' She raised her fingers to her temple again. 'He's correcting me...' She inhaled through her nose, sighed it out of her mouth. 'That's right. He's with your aunt in the spirit world, but he's protective of you both.'

'Oh.' Fiona said this flatly. 'Can I ask him something?' She wiped her face. 'Can I ask where he left the key?'

'The key?'

Fiona stared at her. 'The key.'

Madam Celia is being tested.

Rio could feel everyone dissecting the silence, could feel the doubt begin to settle disappointingly in.

Madam Celia shut her eyes, as if attempting to recentre herself. 'Hmm,' she said awkwardly. 'Hmm.'

'If I may,' G. Alexander said. 'As an international clairvoyant, I'm concerned by what's going on here.' He looked at Fiona and then at Madam Celia. His face was stern, serious. Rio was about to ask what he meant by 'international clairvoyant', but he quickly continued, 'It's obvious you can't answer that question.'

Madam Celia mouthed wordlessly at him, like a fish gulping air.

His voice was quite commanding, now that he had the floor. 'You can't ask something so specific.' He was speaking directly to Fiona now. 'That's just not how it works. I can see Madam Celia is trying her best not to fail you, but spirits just don't communicate in that way; you can't interview them. This isn't an interview.' He turned to Madam Celia, who only gawked at him. 'Madam Celia?' he pressed. 'Do you agree?'

When she did speak, it was with caution. 'Yes. That's right. I'm only a channel for the world beyo—'

'We're vessels for information to move through.' He said this quite passionately, demonstrating it with a forward motion of his hands.

'I'm sorry.' Fiona looked mortified. 'I didn't mean to come across as combative.'

'It's all right,' he said haughtily. 'If you didn't know, then I won't hold it against you.'

'I didn't.' She glanced at Daniel, as if hoping for some support, but he ignored her.

Madam Celia began to blink rapidly. 'Excuse me,' she said. 'This isn't how I conduct my sessions, actually.' She sounded flustered. 'I think things have got off track. I think we should all refocus. Let's everybody close our eyes and concentrate.'

The candles in the middle of the table flickered.

G. Alexander held up his hand. 'A moment please, Celia,' he announced. 'There's someone else here with us who wants our attention.' He gestured just over his shoulder. 'Do you sense them?'

Daniel scanned the area of the room that G. Alexander had just indicated.

'*Madam* Celia,' she said.

It's important that Madam Celia retain authority in the room at all times.

G. Alexander looked at her with something like impatience.

She continued, 'And I really think—'

'Perhaps they're not coming through for you?' he said wryly. And then, to Daniel, 'Some of us are blessed with stronger gifts than others.'

Madam Celia snorted. 'I beg your pardon?'

Who is G. Alexander?

'Can I ask,' Rio said. Everyone turned to look at her. 'Why are you here, Mr Alexander? Was it your intention to hijack Madam Celia's séance?'

Madam Celia began nodding furiously.

'Goodness me, no.' G. Alexander appeared scandalised. 'I moved nearby recently and saw her services advertised in a Costa. I suppose I just wanted to check out my competition; but my intention, of course, was only ever to observe.'

Madam Celia, aghast at what he'd just admitted to, cried, 'So you're an interloper!'

'I have the greatest respect for you.' There was an insincerity to his voice as he reached across the table to touch her hand, but she snatched it away.

'Just what the hell is happening?' Daniel demanded then. 'This is utterly ridiculous. I didn't come here tonight to watch two people bicker.'

Fiona was nodding now, her hands at her face.

'I can assure you my sessions are never normally like this.' Madam Celia looked at them all pleadingly; hairy caterpillars of mascara were now smudged beneath her eyes.

Rio could hear the distress in her voice, and to a degree, felt sorry for her.

'Quiet, please.' G. Alexander suddenly straightened in his chair, alert, like a dog on scent. 'There's a child here.'

'Get out,' Madam Celia said. 'Get out, now.'

Daniel stared at him. 'What?'

'I'm getting the letter M.'

'I mean it,' Madam Celia said. 'I don't permit you to stay at my table.'

'Let him talk,' Daniel said hastily.

Fiona, clearly confused, said to G. Alexander, 'Do you mean Marcus?'

'No. It's ...' G. Alexander closed his eyes, as if intently

concentrating, and then, 'You, sir!' He clasped Daniel firmly on the shoulder. 'It's you!'

'Molly.' Daniel said this like a statement of fact rather than a question. 'My daughter.'

G. Alexander nodded and smiled, delighted, as if someone had just whispered something amusing in his ear. 'She's a lovely little girl,' he said. 'Quite funny. And very interested in things, very curious about what's going on around her.'

The things he was saying sounded vague to Rio, like generalisations and guesswork. In fact, it seemed the whole evening had been based on chance, throwing something out into the dark just to see where it landed.

'She's very sweet-natured, isn't she?' G. Alexander said. 'Very playful. She likes being outside and, that's right, I'm getting music, a tune. Does that make sense to you?'

'Birdsong.' Daniel sounded stunned. 'We liked to identify birds.'

'And I'm getting – I'm getting a smell, like nature. Soil.'

'Yes.' Daniel's voice caught; his hands were shaking.

It all suddenly felt very grotesque. It was obvious that Daniel was grieving and that in coming here, this grief had made him hopeful – blindly so – that something might come of this farce tonight. Even more clear to Rio was that his desperation was being taken advantage of, and it seemed immoral to just sit there and watch it unfold; but then, Rio was being paid to get a story, and that meant observing rather than involving herself.

'I'm getting a real sense of love. A very deep love. The two of you were a unit. You were attached at the hip.'

Daniel began to cry.

'She wants to speak to you directly,' G. Alexander said. 'She wants me to channel her.'

G. Alexander is raising the stakes.

'What?' Madam Celia's voice was sharp. 'Are you sure she doesn't just want to relay a message instead?'

'Is Marcus still around?' Fiona asked. 'Aren't we still talking to him?'

'I can only channel one spirit at a time, my dear,' said G. Alexander.

'*Mr Alexander,*' Madam Celia said sternly, 'I have to *insist* that you *don't.*'

If he heard her, then he pretended not to. He stretched his arms out on the table in front of him, placing his palms on either side of the half-extinguished candles, and then he closed his eyes and began to pant like a dog.

Fiona looked frightened. 'What's happening? What's he doing that for?'

'This is *my* session.' Madam Celia sounded harassed. 'These people have come here for *my* help.'

He only panted louder, chin tipped to his chest. When he began to groan, the hair prickled on Rio's arms.

'Hey,' Madam Celia said loudly.

No one so much as glanced at her.

'*Hey!*' She leaned across the table and shook G. Alexander's arm. He fell silent, swaying slightly in his seat.

'Is he in a trance?' Fiona whispered.

His head jerked up, and he began to slowly retract his hands along the table; the movement was juddery, his palms sticking slightly to the surface. He opened his eyes. For a moment, only the whites were visible. Fiona made a strange, sickened kind of noise, as they began to roll absurdly in their sockets.

G. Alexander started to flutter his eyelids, as if coming to. Madam Celia, looking utterly repulsed by the spectacle of it – *Madam Celia does not like to be upstaged* – got suddenly to her feet, pushing the chair forcefully out from under her so that it clattered to the floor. Daniel and Fiona gaped at her. 'It's Molly,' she cried, holding her fingers to her temple. 'She's saying it isn't working. The energy in the room isn't – it isn't strong enough.'

Madam Celia is taking back her throne.

G. Alexander faltered; his fluttering slowed to blinks. Despite being in the throes of a possession, annoyance was clearly visible in his face.

'She's feeling weakened,' Madam Celia said. 'She has to leave.'

'No.' Daniel was rising from his chair. 'Wait, I want to know if she's all right. I want to know why I can't feel her around me like' – he pointed at Fiona – 'she does with that man.'

'His name is Marcus,' Fiona said.

'She's just *gone*.' Daniel sounded despairing. 'It isn't fair.'

'There!' G. Alexander leapt out of his chair, knocking into the table as he pointed out the window, the remaining candles snuffing themselves out so that the room was flooded suddenly in deepest shadow, and as he did so, Rio got quickly to her feet to see what he was gesturing at, and didn't notice her phone fall directly into the cauldron of tea, submerged entirely.

'Oh my God,' Fiona said. 'What is that?'

It had grown entirely dark outside, so dark that even the nearby gravestones were no longer visible. Out in the distance was a light, singular and small, bouncing low across the meadow, luminous and slowly meandering.

'A spirit,' G. Alexander said, with something like astonishment, as if he couldn't quite believe it himself.

'It's heading to the woods,' Madam Celia said. 'I've long sensed it's a place where spirits gather.'

Daniel turned and ran out the front door, presumably to follow the light, leaving his coat slung on the chair.

'Do you think he'll catch up to it?' Fiona asked. 'It's quite far away.'

'I doubt it even matters if he does, you know,' G. Alexander said quietly.

Whereas the others appeared to be in awe of what had occurred, Rio found herself unsettled. It wasn't that she'd been let down by the evening – she'd not expected to be convinced, not really. It was, she realised, Daniel that bothered her, his futile hope; it was wilful irrationality that had him running from the room just now, driven by nothing but a fantasy.

She moved closer to the window and watched Daniel running out into the dark, and in the far distance, the orb seemed to grow momentarily brighter, before it disappeared as quickly as if someone had flicked a switch.

Nell

Nell had always longed to steal the kingfisher.

She was alone in Oonagh's front room with the door shut, sat on the loveseat and still in her woollen coat, which was far too long for her, too wide in the shoulders; it gave her the air of a child playing dress-up, although she was soon to be eighty-three. But it was a practical item, one she'd had nearly twenty years, with large pockets containing any strange assortment of things – sticky plasters and pens, for example, a small tub of Vaseline, tealights, a pack of cards. There were so many people milling about the rest of the house – people Nell didn't know – that the back door had to be kept open for them to spill out into the garden, and because it was the cusp of October and the temperature was starting to cool despite the drought, Nell had decided to keep the coat on.

She could still hear Judy buzzing around the kitchen, her voice both loud and muffled at once, making pleasantries and offerings, as if this were a party and it were her house. It annoyed Nell; Judy annoyed Nell. She'd spent a tedious hour watching Judy faff, unwrapping yet more cellophaned dishes of food that people had brought in condolence, even though there was already too much out and it would be better kept in the fridge for Walter, for later, or put into the freezer for use in the ensuing days and weeks and months of adjustment. Judy, like everyone else, had kept cloyingly close to Walter, which meant that Nell could not say the things she wanted to him, things that she meant sincerely and wanted to express in private. And when she could no longer bear Judy trying to make her do things – *Nell, would you see if anyone needs a drink?* – Nell had retreated to the living room, where it was far less isolating to be than it was out there with all of them.

Nell did not particularly care that she was being antisocial. She was comfortable in this room, couldn't even hazard a guess at how many times she'd sat in this very spot with Oonagh, next to a bookshelf that was stuffed to its edges. Oonagh had often said that she liked to collect evidence of a life lived well. There were souvenirs and trinkets, vases of flowers she had dried from the garden, paintings she'd done of the places she'd visited: Cornish cliffs, a Japanese pagoda bordered with actual cherry blossoms pressed from her trip, a pastel-hued village in Santorini. There was an ornate coffee table from some far-flung market, an antique writing bureau in the corner that had once belonged to someone apparently impressive but whose name Nell didn't recognise, and more lamps than were necessary, all of them covered in various patterned fabrics that she'd collected on her travels and somehow matched to colours in the rug. Nell slid her stockinged feet over it now, thick-piled and soft.

And then there was the loveseat. Oonagh had reupholstered it herself, years ago now, as Nell kept her company. It would have been a somewhat unremarkable afternoon (it was the unremarkable afternoons that Nell would miss the most), the hours of chitchat punctuated now and then by the sound of the staple gun as Oonagh attached a new red damask to the back of the loveseat. But then Oonagh had gone and stapled her finger to the frame, and screamed, hysterical – overreacting, really – and Nell, hardly thinking at all, quite calmly fetched a pair of pliers from her coat pocket and yanked it out. And Oonagh, sat as she was in the middle of the floor, holding her bleeding finger above her head, laughed at the unexpected revelation that Nell of all people had been walking around with pliers in her pocket for no discernible reason – *Pliers? What on earth are* you *carrying around pliers for!* – laughed so hard she'd cried. Nell, who couldn't see what was so funny, thought Oonagh must have been in shock; she'd left the pliers there with her, just in case it happened again.

Nell's flat in the retirement home was nothing like Oonagh's house, was not colourful and warm, or even very full, did not feel how a home ought to – welcoming and cosy – the way this did, which was why Nell had always insisted they get together here. Nell could not decorate a room the way Oonagh could, did not have the same eye or knowhow, had not travelled and accumulated things to fill it with, had never even lived beyond a forty-mile radius of Norwich, where she was born and raised, whereas she was sure that Oonagh had said she'd lived in Spain for a time in her youth, and had been born in Scotland. The closest Nell had ever come to experiencing other cultures had been through two of the staff at the retirement home, Riverside House: Andrei, who'd shown her how to make proper Romanian cabbage rolls in clay pots, and tripe soup served with sour cream; and there was Lipa, who had them all crafting traditional Polish ornaments at Christmas – little animals made from dough, hand formed and cooked, and brightly coloured paper chandeliers to festoon the entryway with, and the tree laden with apples and biscuits; but they were both back in Europe now, made to leave after the UK's withdrawal, and the care home was the poorer for it, was still having trouble finding new staff to replace them. She'd tried adorning her flat the way Oonagh might, picking the odd ornament up when she was out shopping, but it wasn't the same; they didn't feel the way Oonagh's things did, which always had a story attached to them – a flea market haggle, for instance, an ancestral connection – and this gave them a certain presence in the room.

Of all the things in Oonagh's house, it was always the kingfisher that captured Nell's attention. It was a piece of taxidermy about the size of her palm and positioned so it was perching on a branch. Oonagh found it dead years ago, she said, at the nearby river, just lying on the bank serenely, as if it had simply given up mid-flight to fall perfectly there on the grass. Oonagh had been so moved by its vibrancy, its perfect beauty, that she'd had it stuffed. It managed to catch the light from the sun or a lamp, making electric its blue and orange feathers, giving it an appearance closer to stained glass or a brilliant jewel than a bird found in Britain.

Nell always thought the kingfisher got lost, tucked away on the shelf as it was, minimised by everything else around it. The poor thing deserved more; its loveliness ought to have been celebrated instead of confined to the corner, half-forgotten with the rest. It occurred to her then, with a sharp and morose understanding, that she would probably never be here again, among all the things as familiar to Nell as if they were her own. Since she'd heard the news of Oonagh's death, it seemed to her that she was sometimes in the centre of a large bubble which would burst every so often, sudden, and shocking, and letting in a desperate sadness; it did that now, and she was glad that she was alone.

Nell caught a whiff of burning cigarette. Oonagh hated that smell, would've hated it being in her house, stinking her things. She thought with some surprise that Walter might not mind it. But then, she didn't know him with the same intimacy; Nell had been Oonagh's friend. That it was Judy, then, who'd been the one to phone and inform her of Oonagh's passing, and not the other way around, was a bitterness that Nell felt keenly. It meant that someone – Walter – must have decided that Judy and not Nell had been the more important friend, the friend who should be told first, who should break the news beyond the family. The worst part, though, was that maybe there was a reason he thought this: that maybe, actually, it was true, and this drop of doubt had seeped in and begun to colour Nell's perception of her years with Oonagh in bitter tones.

Nell got slowly to her feet, bracing her knuckles ungracefully against the seat cushion, and went to the kingfisher.

She'd decided long ago that it was pointing towards the river, as if directing her attention there, the way its back was so straight, and its beak so sharp and like a compass needle. From so close, she could see the imbrication of its feathers, see each barbarous fibre of its plumage.

She began to stroke it; the feathers were like silk beneath her fingers, cool and smooth, but coated with a finely granular dust from having sat, untouched, for so long. And then, not quite by impulse, she took the kingfisher firmly in her hand, fingers wrapped around its little body, and pulled hard. It came off the branch easily and she paused, not entirely certain what she'd done and why. She considered it briefly – there were thin wire posts sticking out from its neon feet – and then put it into her coat pocket. A swell of adrenalin seized her, and she hurried out of the room and through the front door, walking as quickly as she could, her head instinctively cast downward, both from caution on the uneven path and from having done something thrillingly illicit. It was not until she turned to close the gate behind her that she saw a young man standing in Oonagh's front garden by the living-room window, and the fluttering that was already in her chest became so compounded by the unexpected sight of him, that an involuntary whimper left her.

He must have realised that he'd startled her, because he said quietly, 'All right?'

His tone, his expression, were of impassive inscrutability. Nell, embarrassed at the noise she'd made, stared at him. He was holding a lit cigarette.

'I hope you put that in the bin when you're done with it, and don't just drop it in the plants,' she said, before pulling her collar tightly around her neck and walking away.

At home, Nell removed the bird from her pocket as if it were still alive, careful not to snag its exquisite feathers on the coarse woollen fabric of her coat and ruin them. She wiped away the dust that covered it with a damp cloth, and then opened the kitchen window and set the kingfisher on the sill to dry in the mild autumnal sun. The walk back from Oonagh's was short, only a few minutes down the road, but she'd felt she couldn't reach her door fast enough, that behind her lay a vague sense of threat. She didn't know how long he'd been there at the window, or what, if anything, he'd seen, but something about this stranger had nipped at her heels as she hastened down the small hill – Norfolk was not *entirely* flat – and crossed the raised pavement over the trickling ford where the road was level with the river, the incline towards the retirement home slowing her down a little, burning her calves, and she was huffing by the time she reached its doors, sweat beading her forehead. Riverside House was on the outskirts of the village, and was a very large and very old Victorian building that had at one time been a workhouse for the poor and needy, but was these days independent living for the elderly. Despite the age of it, her flat was lacking in character, the renovations undertaken to transform it in the sixties having rendered it sterile, and all the rooms small and painted a dreary magnolia. But it had lovely light in the mornings, and it was on the top floor, which meant fewer of those ugly handrails screwed into the walls and long red emergency cords hanging in every room, like in the flats on the ground floor where they put all of the people that they wanted to keep an eye on. In the safety of her little home, she was calmer, surer in her anonymity. The man didn't know who she was, wouldn't even know her name.

When at last she sat at the kitchen table, sipping her tea gratefully, she realised that she'd not said goodbye, and wondered if Judy might call later to ask why she'd gone so abruptly. She'd have to feign nausea or a migraine, and say she'd come home to lie down. In fact, she was sure that Judy would call. Nell's mother had been of the same disposition, made it her business to know everyone else's. They hadn't been able to afford a television – not many people in their area could at the time – and Nell suspected that interfering was her mother's form of entertainment. She'd not been a cruel woman, but she'd been critical in her opinions and careless with how she shared them, and she often made Nell feel inadequate. She'd regularly compared Nell to other girls of a similar age, girls who were always better in some way. Occasionally it was done under the guise of aspirational self-improvement, and at other times a visible irritation that her only daughter was somehow deficient.

After a while in the sun, a little heat was held in the kingfisher's feathers, and Nell appreciated the sensation of it in her palm, pleasant and reassuring, as if it were still warm-blooded. Its feathers were glossier now they weren't covered with a layer of dust. It was a shame about the wire posts, though, protruding from its delicate feet; it meant the kingfisher was unable to stand upright, and the sight of them detracted from its diminutive magnificence. The posts were not something she could get rid of herself (she'd never got her pliers back from Oonagh) and so she phoned down for Paul, the handyman, who brought his tools up with him an hour later.

'Bit far from the river, isn't it?' he quipped, holding it up to the window and turning it in his hand like a precious stone (even though Nell had made him wash his hands before touching the kingfisher, he still had crescents of dirt beneath his fingernails). He was a large man, tall and broad, with a somewhat unruly beard and jolly eyes, and he was almost always in a flat cap.

'You know what it is?'

'Well, sure.' He snipped one of the posts and it ricocheted against the wall. 'Me and my boys see them all the time when we're fishing.'

'Is that right?' she said. 'Maybe I should get myself to the river. Maybe I should take up birdwatching.'

'They're too quick. By the time you'd raised your binoculars they'd be halfway down the bleedin' Wensum. It's a bit like watching for lightning and blinking when it hits.'

'I've never seen one alive, though I've always thought this one felt animated in some way, its face ... I don't know, like it might wink at me,' she said happily.

'I see what you mean,' he said. 'It's got some character to it.'

'Exactly.'

'And I'll tell you something,' he said, snipping off the other post. 'Their feathers aren't actually blue at all, they're a dull brown. It's just a trick of the light.' He picked the errant pieces of metal off the floor and put them in his pocket.

'Well,' she said, impressed. 'I didn't know that.'

She'd never given much thought to Paul. She'd seen him around often enough, weeding the rose beds outside or repairing the picture rail in the entryway, and though he'd been in her flat before to stop a leak beneath her kitchen sink, she'd not once considered that he might, like her, appreciate beautiful things.

'It's a right lovely creature,' he said admiringly, as he handed the kingfisher back to Nell.

'Yes,' she said proudly, 'it is.'

After he'd gone, she placed the kingfisher on a shelf in the living room. Because its feet had been made to curl around a branch, she had to lean it against a Tuscan-inspired tile that she'd once bought from a charity shop in Holt, to stop the poor thing falling over. Positioned among the ordinariness of her belongings – the tile, a small potted cactus that made her think of the Arizonian desert but actually came from Tesco, some razor clam shells from a Norfolk beach (Gorleston-on-Sea or Sheringham, probably) – it looked odd, incongruous in its beauty, and she was discouraged that it hadn't immediately elevated the rest of her things, and was sure that were it the other way around, had any of her possessions been transplanted to Oonagh's home, then they would have become transformed, made lovelier simply by their proximity to Oonagh's belongings. *They're just things, Nellie*, Oonagh had been fond of saying as she showed off something else newly acquired. *They don't mean anything, really.* Nell had always found it insincere and placating when Oonagh made comments like this, though she'd never said so.

It was strange to think that only a couple of hours before, she'd been at her friend's memorial. It wasn't yet teatime, but Nell, overcome with fatigue, decided she would get into bed, and drew the curtains against the last residue of daylight. It took her a long time to drift into sleep, sure that Judy would call to talk about poor Oonagh and the sudden noise of the phone would startle her, and she spent the hours somewhere between there and awake, pulled repeatedly from the drowsy current of slumber by the shrill two-noted whistle of a bird.

When the telephone did ring the following day, it was not Judy, but the vicar, Rev. Eileen Wright, asking if she might come round that afternoon for a quick visit between meetings. She did this every so often, and while she didn't ever say it was because she thought Nell might be a bit lonely, Nell knew that it was the unspoken reason and was always grateful (if a little resentful) of the company. Nell went to church every Sunday, though if she were being honest, she wasn't particularly fussed by the sermons, which were always in some way about being good to one another. Really, she went because of the people that made up Eileen's parish, who were pleasant and sent get well soon cards to her if she was poorly, and because there was always a few of them who lingered after for a natter, always someone chatting about something going on in one of the neighbouring hamlets.

And she liked Eileen, who organised quiz nights and movie nights, and lectures at the church when the weather was warm enough to sit comfortably within its cool flint walls. Sometimes Oonagh, who hadn't gone to church as regularly as Nell, would attend these events with her, and they'd whisper asides to one another, giggling disruptively.

When Eileen arrived, Nell made sure that her guest was sat facing the kingfisher, in the same way she'd always done at Oonagh's, when she'd had to admire from a distance what she coveted. She wondered if Eileen would covet it too, once she saw how lovely the kingfisher was, even though vicars were presumably not allowed to feel envy. Nell might let her hold it, if her hands were clean and she promised to be careful with its feathers. She had fashioned a branch out of rolled-up paper for the kingfisher to perch on. It was more alive, now that it was standing up independently, unaided by the tile.

Eileen had a kind, inquisitive face, younger than Nell (she guessed in her sixties) and plump-cheeked, with blue eyes and a thick cloud of greying blonde hair on her shoulders, a small mouth that unfortunately did not hide her crooked eye tooth. She sat with her hands clasped politely together on her lap, as if waiting to sing a hymn in choir.

'Would you like any tea?' Nell said.

'I can't stay long at all today, I'm afraid.' Eileen looked apologetic. 'But how are you, Ms Riley?'

'Oh fine,' Nell said. 'Fine.' Her eyes were on the kingfisher, hoping the vicar might follow suit. And then (because she could not forget her manners, no matter how excited or impatient she'd become), 'And how are you?'

Eileen sort of shrugged, as if she didn't know how she was. 'I suppose I'm very well, thank you.' She still hadn't looked across the room.

'Apparently they're halting the development,' Nell said, making conversation. 'So that's good, isn't it? They'd not been at it long.'

'Yes, well,' Eileen said, 'pausing it, for now. Too many injuries on site, as I'm sure you're aware.'

Nell had overheard a conversation about it in Oonagh's hallway as she retreated to the living room yesterday, catching only that it was stopping and no other details, before shutting the door behind her. 'What kind of injuries?'

Eileen pulled a face, as if she found the question unpleasant. 'Bad ones. Caldwell claim they're doing everything by the book, but of course they'd say that. They've to wait for a Health and Safety investigation before they can start again, so fingers crossed they're permanently shut down. In fact, I wonder if it wouldn't be a good idea rallying the troops to see if we can't take the opportunity to make our case again. The council might listen this time, if the site is hazardous. I think it's worth getting together for another meeting.'

Nell thought the spate of injuries could be the curse of Old Hesket, but she didn't know if it was in some way blasphemous to try to engage a vicar in that kind of talk. And anyway, the last time she'd brought it up had been with Oonagh's neighbour, Isla (weeks ago, in those days before Oonagh's passing), who she'd found – rather oddly – just sat on the pavement one afternoon, and who'd seemed more bemused by the curse than concerned, as if Nell were nothing but a dotty old woman. 'It's been quite a drought, hasn't it?' she said instead. 'Very unusual for autumn?'

'We've had prolonged summers before, but it does feel like we should've had *some* rain by now. It's concerning how early the trees have been losing their leaves because of it.'

Nell deliberately spoke to the kingfisher, trying to direct Eileen's attention. 'I expect people think it's because of climate change.'

'As opposed to what?'

Nell paused, unsure of how to continue. She didn't really care about the weather; she only wanted Eileen to notice the kingfisher without having to point it out to her, which would be a crass thing to do, like she was showing off. Oonagh had never needed to show off (Nell always spotted a new treasure), but she had a habit of steering the conversation – *In that case, you might appreciate this vase, Nellie* – in a way that Nell was sure she'd never done with anyone else, maybe because she knew it wouldn't vex someone like Judy, who had so much money and such insipid taste, how it would Nell.

'I ran into Linda on my way in,' Eileen said. Linda was the retirement home manager; Nell had little patience for Linda, who was always smiling (even if there was nothing to smile about, so that it seemed quite performative), and always talked to the residents as if *everything* was exciting news. It was all very infantilising. 'She's such a lovely woman,' Eileen continued. 'I really respect how much she cares for the residents here. She has a great deal of concern for your wellbeing, you know, what with everything you've gone through lately. It's good she's around to look after you.'

'I look after myself,' Nell bristled. 'I've told her that I'm getting on fine.'

Eileen smiled benevolently. 'Of course you are, Ms Riley.'

Nell had suddenly grown tired of waiting. 'Did you know that kingfishers aren't really blue?'

Eileen frowned, as if thrown by the question. 'The birds?'

'Only I found one.'

'You *found* one? Where?'

'Aylsham,' Nell lied.

Eileen considered Nell a moment, her head cocked. 'You know, I saw Walter Moody this morning.'

Nell could hear the shift in how the vicar spoke, the subtle change in tone, and she had the uneasy sense that something was coming.

'He was ...' Eileen paused, sifted for the word. 'He was troubled.'

'Well,' Nell said, 'his wife has died.'

'Yes,' Eileen said patiently, 'but we were speaking about you.'

She felt suddenly wrong-footed, as though she had been lulled falsely into this meeting. Out of the corner of her eye, a sudden small movement – no more than a twitch – caught her attention, and she spun to see the kingfisher, stood lifelessly on the shelf.

'He said you just sort of vanished yesterday,' Eileen continued. 'His grandson saw you leave quite abruptly.'

There was a horrid sensation in Nell's ribcage, like a great big fish thrashing on land, desperate to get itself back into the river. She was conscious of keeping her voice placid, her face unimpeachable. The young man standing outside Oonagh's house, stinking the place out with his cigarettes. She had quite forgotten about him in the time since she'd left the house, which felt an erroneous, cavalier thing to have done, now that she was sitting here, unprepared.

'I'm sure you can understand that Walter is quite upset at the moment.' Eileen put her hand on Nell's forearm. 'I'm sure that you are as well. I'm sure that's why—' She glanced then, finally, at the kingfisher, and it was clear in that moment she'd been avoiding looking at it, that she knew exactly where it had come from.

Nell's mortification was immediate and severe. She wondered, briefly, if she might be sick on herself.

Eileen quietly cleared her throat. 'Walter wants to see you.'

'Is that what he said?' Nell's own voice sounded distant to her. 'What about?'

Eileen squeezed her arm gently. 'I'm awfully sorry it's been such a flying visit, Ms Riley, but I'm meeting a couple about a christening in twenty minutes.'

Nell walked in a stupor to the front door with Eileen trailing behind her, saying something – possibly about coming back again soon – that Nell could hardly register for the way her thoughts were spinning. Eileen touched Nell's shoulder, and then was gone. As Nell returned to the living room, she clocked immediately that the kingfisher was now gone as well, absent from its paper perch, and her fears came at once, rapid-fire and tumbling: that the vicar had taken it, that she was on her way to return it to Walter as proof of Nell's duplicity, and soon everyone would know what she had done and what a terrible friend to Oonagh she was. She had to grip the back of the settee to steady herself, panic kicking uncontrollably within her until, in a moment of intense relief, she saw it plainly on the floor, only fallen.

Over the next few days her mind winged in erratic loops. She could imagine him vividly – Oonagh's grandson, Jack – lingering with his cigarette, spying on her through the window. She'd not recognised him from the pictures framed about the house, had not realised he was so old as that now. He'd probably gone inside after she'd left and told them all, announced to the whole memorial the crime she had committed. Perhaps that's why Judy hadn't called her yet (she couldn't bear the thought of Judy having this over her!). Perhaps no one wanted to associate with her any more. Walter would no doubt be hurt; furious. As she went on like this, unendingly returning to the encounter in her mind, regret – no, it was stronger: shame, guilt – began to tarnish the kingfisher. She could no longer admire it the way she had for so long. It had taken on an unpleasant quality overnight, tainted now in a grotesque kind of disgrace. Even when she sat reading on the sofa or watching something on the television, there it was on the shelf, the kingfisher and its implications on the fringes of her awareness, its shiny black eyes looking out into the room, its dissecting, cold stare. More and more, she thought she glimpsed its small body shuddering in her periphery, making her jump, filling her with unease, though of course it hadn't actually moved – of course not! – but still, there were times immediately after that she picked up the phone in a fright to call Oonagh, remembering only as she was dialling the number how the kingfisher had been procured in the first place and, worse, that it would be Walter who answered anyway, Walter who knew of her thievery. And each time came the dreadful realisation that really, now, she had no one to confide in, with Oonagh gone.

Sometimes she found the bird inexplicably on the floor; on one occasion it was in the middle of the room, as though she'd caught it midway to the door. Its stuffing must be making it unbalanced, she rationalised, or else it was the unstable way its feet were positioned curling inwards, her makeshift branch not a good enough support, so she moved the little Tesco cactus in front of the kingfisher to wedge it in.

Finally, one morning, she decided that she'd simply spent too much time in her own company, that a lack of socialisation was making her jumpy, playing with her head, and she phoned downstairs for Paul. He was just about to get on with clearing the gutters, so she made up an excuse that one of the light bulbs in her flat needed changing, even though they were the LED kind and meant to last years, and he sighed, saying that it was a good thing then that she'd just got him before he'd gone up the ladder.

When she showed him into the kitchen, he flicked the light switch on and off, and saw that it was working. She waited as he tried the hallway switch, and then did the same in the bathroom opposite.

'Which one is it, then?'

'I've made you a cup of tea.'

'Oh.' He appeared surprised. 'Oh, right.' He picked it up – 'Cheers' – and took a sip, but it was scalding still, and he winced, putting it back down on the table.

She pushed the plate of shortbread towards him.

'Go on then.' He winked as he took a bite, then gestured to the bedroom and said with his mouth full, 'Is it through there?' Crumbs fell into his beard.

'Can't you sit for a bit?' she protested. 'You're not in a rush, are you?'

But he was already in the hallway again, and she rose, following him.

'Full-on day today, Ms Riley.' He tried the bedroom light, watched it flick on and then off. 'I'm installing some new shelves in the utility room once those gutters are done.' He walked ahead of her and tried the living-room light, which was of course working. He turned to her, frowning.

'I didn't realise you were quite so busy,' she said apologetically. She thought he'd be cross with her for wasting his time, but it was worse.

'It can be hard, feeling lonely sometimes.' His expression was pitying, his voice overly consoling. 'I can at least stay long enough to finish my tea.'

A pulsing heat in the cartilage of her ears. 'No, no. It's fine, really.' She'd rather he left if this was how it was going to be, if he was going to feel sorry for her.

He stooped to pick up the kingfisher, which was again on the floor. This time, the cactus she'd carefully positioned to keep it from falling had been knocked off too, jettisoned from its tin pot to land by the sofa, a spray of soil across the carpet. 'I'll get this cleaned up first,' he said.

She took the kingfisher from him reluctantly. It stared balefully, its eyes gleaming and black, and in them, to her intense shock, was a minute face gazing back at her – Oonagh's face – and as her heart leapt in fright, she felt an impossible movement of feather straining at her thumb, and flung the kingfisher to the floor again, recoiling.

'Are you all right, Ms Riley?'

'I—' But as she stood there, unblinking, watching how inanimate it was, how dead after all; she decided it must have only been her pulse beating hard through muscle and skin, and that the image she'd seen was only herself reflected. 'I'm fine.'

'Are you sure?' Her behaviour had concerned him, that much was clear.

'Clumsy me.' She said this as airily as she could manage, knowing that she ought to pick up the kingfisher and make a joke of what she'd just done. But she was too repulsed by the idea of touching it again to do anything but apologise to Paul, who continued to look worriedly at her, until she left the room.

She couldn't throw it away, not when it had belonged to Oonagh.

Later, in the bath, the water clattering as the tub continued to fill around her, she heard a noise against the bathroom door, a dull but distinct knock. Startled, her first thought was that Paul had left something behind and let himself in to retrieve it.

'Hello?' she called.

Another knocking, more forceful now.

She covered herself with her hands (there were no locks on any of the bathrooms in case a resident slipped and needed assistance), craning her head over the side of the tub and away from the racket of the running tap. 'Is someone there?' she said, louder. 'Paul?'

A scrabbling noise, the door quivering slightly in its frame, and a quiet fretting sound from in the hallway, like the flipping of a book's pages.

Like the flapping of small wings.

A fear then, overwhelmingly intense. 'Go away,' she cried. 'Go away, you horrible thing!'

The sound became more frantic, battering against the wood, determined to get in, battering and battering. Instinctively, she reached for the tap to turn it off so that she could listen better, and just as abruptly, the noise outside stopped and there was only silence.

Trembling, she sat in the bath, staring at the door. When it remained unmoving after some fraught moments, she rose slowly from the water and stood dripping on the mat, trying to calm herself. There would be a rational explanation. The disturbance she'd heard had only been the sound of the tub filling, or maybe she'd opened the kitchen window for some air and forgotten to close it again, and the wind ... But logic was quick to turn on her, mutinous and unwieldly, and she became certain that whatever was happening at the door was real, and that the source of her torment was wholly an unnatural one. She needed to get to her phone; she had to call for Paul or the police. Cautiously, Nell inched the door open, terrified that she'd find the bird there and it would fly at her, that its claws would rip into her skin, its beak gouge her eyes, that it would tangle itself in her hair and tear her scalp to bits.

The hallway, however, was empty.

She draped a bath towel over her head like a cloak and ventured cautiously to her bedroom. It could be hiding anywhere, small as it was, waiting to dart at her.

But as she tiptoed past the living room, scanning madly for a sudden flash of blue, she saw it there, rigid on the shelf again behind the newly re-potted cactus, just as Paul had left it.

It was almost anticlimactic, how quickly the fear fell away at the sight of the kingfisher, unmoving and stiff as it was meant to be, and now that all terror had gone, she stood there, naked and incensed. 'What do you *want*?' she shouted shrilly. 'Don't you have anything better to do?'

The solution came to her, fully formed and with such a lucidity, that she wondered if it had somehow been communicated to her: the kingfisher didn't want to be there, in her flat; it wanted to be returned home. Before she could lose her nerve, she threw on her coat and put the kingfisher again in her pocket, and went. In the lobby, Paul and Linda were standing together, talking in hushed voices; it must have been a serious conversation because, for once, Linda was not smiling. As she passed them, Nell was certain she heard Paul say something about a bird, was sure they watched her as she left the building.

The sun was bright and high, the sky free of the heavy clouds that had lately hung over Hesket but never released their rain, and now that she was outside, away from the confines of her flat, she was compelled forward by the loveliness of the day, but more so by the thought of distancing herself from Paul and Linda back at Riverside House, and the sinking feeling which trailed after her, that soon enough they'd move her to the ground floor. As she walked, she entertained the idea of knocking on Walter's door and bravely admitting to what she'd done before apologising. But she knew that she could not; she would post the kingfisher through the letterbox and leave without a word, like a coward.

She walked past all the dry lawns with their cracked patches of bare earth and wilted, shrivelled plants, their crisp piles of autumn-shed leaves, and the houses, all of them displaying ugly posters protesting the development, and cars lined up along the road in front of them. When at last she got to Walter's wooden gate, she hesitated only momentarily, before pushing it open.

'Nell?'

She turned. Walter was getting out of his car.

'There you are,' he said. 'I was wondering when I might see you.' He walked to her, keys dangling in his hand. 'Are you coming inside? I want a word.'

It was as though all the breath had left her. 'No, I ...'

He glanced at her hand on the gate, and she removed it quickly, self-consciously, and reached now into her pocket; better to get it done swiftly, push it into his hands and walk away.

'Mind yourself on that.' He gestured to the gate and then showed Nell his palms. 'I keep getting splinters from it. Got another one this morning. I haven't been able to remove all of it either. You can see where it's still there, look.' He moved his hand closer to her face. 'I don't suppose you've brought more pliers with you.'

That he was joking surprised Nell. 'I'd left them with Oonagh.' She was holding the kingfisher at her side, her fist closed tightly around its little body, its long, thin beak protruding from between her fingers.

'I know,' he said. 'The little magpie kept them on her dressing table. I always thought it looked a bit funny, having them next to her perfume bottles. But you know how she liked to collect things with a story behind them.' He smiled sadly. 'I can get them for you if you like. Are you sure you won't come in?'

She raised the kingfisher and held it between them both; she would do it now. 'Walter, I—'

He suddenly enclosed the whole of her hand in both of his, the act startling Nell, so that she recoiled a little. 'You know,' Walter said softly, 'she always admired your ability to surprise her. She'd say that if someone were to look at her friend Nell and didn't know her, they'd be in danger of thinking she was just another old lady like her.'

She was aware, vaguely, of the kingfisher's claws sharp

against her fleshy palm, of a trembling sensation coming from its body – or was it her own? She was no longer sure.

'I've always known how much you've admired Oonagh's things.' His hands were hot and encompassing, and he held on to her, to the kingfisher, a few moments more, before letting go. 'Please come round again soon, won't you? I make a very good cup of tea.'

It was a longer walk than Nell was used to, but she took her time, making her way carefully across the uneven meadow until she reached the river, far from where anyone could really see her. The sun hit sharply on its mirrored surface, reflecting the light into her eyes. She steadied herself against the gnarled trunk of an oak tree that overhung the water and reached into her pocket as the wind hissed through the trees.

'Right,' she said to the kingfisher, 'away with you now. Go back to where you belong.'

And then she swung her arm and opened her hand, so that the kingfisher was thrown out and far into the river, and as it arced towards the water that shimmered with the current and the sun, like so many pieces of glitter, its wings seemed to spread in a brilliant blue flare, ochre belly stretching and rising, and Nell, who could not help but blink at the glaring light, wasn't sure if what she'd seen was right or true, whether the kingfisher had gone under and left only ripples on the surface, or had indeed beat away along the river, beneath the vibrant blue sky, until it was nothing at all.

Jack

The rowan tree at the end of the garden had been steadily dying for some time. Its cankerous bark was peeling like a scroll, revealing wood so blackened in places it looked to have been charred by fire, and its trunk was riddled with fungi in brackets of tough grey shelves and soft-looking folds of yellow. Jack's granny, Oonagh, had loved that tree, had spent so many springs reading beneath its creamy froth of blossom or watching the blackbirds feast on its scarlet berries in autumn, and since she was now gone, his grandpa Walter refused to cut it down. And so it'd stood there, creaking even in the slightest wind, full of decay and ready to topple at any time, until finally Jack took his chainsaw to it while Walter was at the allotment, and that was that. All that remained of it was a stump.

'It was dangerous,' Jack explained over a cup of tea at the kitchen table. 'Next strong wind would've had it.' He showed him a piece of the trunk to demonstrate just how rotten it was, but Walter, sullen, only examined his own hands on the table edge in front of him, still filthy from the allotment (his grandpa's hands were always this way now, soil-coated, unwashed). Jack moved the wood closer, trying to show him the way it easily fell apart when he flicked at it with his fingernail, but stubbornly, Walter turned his cheek as quickly as if he'd been slapped. It was a petulant thing to do, looking away like that, and his behaviour surprised Jack. Since Oonagh's death, Walter had grown more withdrawn, which was partly why Jack had moved into the spare room for a while, to keep him company, help him adjust, but this – his brooding – was something else. Jack put the piece of wood on the table, and even though he knew the answer, he asked the question anyway. 'Are you in a mood with me now?'

After a silence, 'No.'

'Because it seems like you are.'

More silence.

'I was only helping.'

'Helping?' Walter sounded incredulous. 'Helping!'

'You couldn't have done it yourself.'

'I didn't want it doing in the first place.' Walter scowled, his voice louder now. 'And I don't appreciate you sneaking around behind my back.'

'That's not what happened.'

'I think it is, actually.' And then Walter stood and walked angrily out of the room, leaving his cup of tea untouched.

After a moment, Jack heard him on the stairs and thought, in a flash of annoyance, that he was going up to sulk. He'd expected, at least, that when Walter came home, he'd be a little appreciative once the shock had worn off. He'd wanted to show his grandpa the growth rings, how impressive it was for a rowan, of all trees, to get to that kind of age. He tipped Walter's tea down the sink, and wiped specks of soil from the tabletop with his palm; Oonagh hadn't abided dirty surfaces. But now she was gone, Jack had noticed coatings of dust on the wood furniture and lamps, rings of pink scum around the taps and drains, spilled food crusted on the kitchen counters. And there had been other things, worrying things – the hob left on unattended, red hot for hours while Walter was at the allotment, or his missing car keys found, finally, shut away in the bathroom cabinet instead of deposited on the little table by the door, a book placed in the fridge on top of the cheese – a newfound absentmindedness. But Jack knew that allowances must be made; his grandpa was grieving, and grief has strange ways.

As Jack rolled himself a cigarette, he entertained the idea that Walter was only pretending to be upset about the tree. Walter had always played tricks, like painting the bar soap with clear nail varnish so that it didn't lather, or Sellotaping the bathroom tap to make it spray water all over whoever turned it on. Jack, of course, did it back. Once, when he was still a teenager (he was twenty-three now), Walter and Oonagh had gone on holiday and Jack turned everything in their house quite literally upside down. *Why can't you two just say I love you, like normal people?* Oonagh had lamented.

But Walter remained taciturnly upstairs, and Jack soon gave up on the hope that his mood was only pretend. His granny would have known what to say to bring him down again; she'd had the ability to explain things in a way that made them each understand the other, and since she'd been gone, the differences that arose between them now went unbridged.

Outside it was trying to rain, but even though the sky looked capable of a downpour, it only managed the mizzling sort that whirled in the air like mist, as if the clouds themselves were one big Sellotaped tap, dousing the grass with pinheaded beads too minuscule, too weightless, to run down the stalks and wet the soil. He hadn't brought a raincoat with him; it'd been an exceedingly dry autumn in Hesket so far, and he'd not had need of one since early summer. He contemplated staying inside a while longer and having another cup of tea but decided against it. The daylight hours were less now that they were midway into October, and the debris still needed clearing from the garden, the logs chopped into firewood.

He found the axe in the shed, heavy-headed and old, and held it at his side while he smoked, knocking the butt of it absentmindedly against his leg. After a short while, Jack crushed the cigarette against the gate to make sure it was out, then flicked it into the meadow. From the end of Walter's garden, by the little fishpond blanketed with weeds, he could still see where the chipper truck had worn snaking tracks beside the allotment (they'd had to remove some of the hedgerow to gain access from the road) and out across the meadow to the edge of the treeline, leaving flattened yellow grasses in its wake. The truck would return as soon as the Health and Safety Executive had concluded its investigation, and everything could start up again.

Jack was looking forward to it.

It was a paycheque, a decent one, and it was hard enough to get on the property ladder with the market the way it was (this had been another reason for his moving in – he could save on rent and put the money towards a house deposit). It had been different in Walter's time, when a house could be bought on a single salary in your twenties, and though Jack would never say it, he thought Walter was being selfish. The woods would be cut down whether Jack was involved or not, so why shouldn't he earn some money out of it? Caldwell & Associates had recently promised the tree surgeons a bonus when the job was done as an incentive to keep people on, and they'd even tried appeasing the villagers, too: the woodchip would go to the parish council (or parish traitors, as Walter called them), who would in turn donate it to the community allotment for use as mulch. Admittedly, Jack didn't understand why the new homes couldn't just be sited on the meadow alone instead of ripping out perfectly good woodland, but who was he to say where things should be built.

Walter had refused to entertain Jack's perspective, and despaired, mostly, over how embarrassing it would be if the village found out his own grandson was in bed with the enemy. He forbade Jack from mentioning it to anyone and insisted that he take an elaborate route to and from work so that no one saw him. Jack had to assure him that in the unlikely event anyone from the village wandered onto the site, they wouldn't recognise him in all that gear anyway, that his face would be obscured by a helmet and visor. This must have placated Walter somewhat, because there'd been nothing since that outburst, and the tension had simmered quietly between them, unaddressed and un-mended, the two of them cohabiting in strained politeness as if they were strangers in a house share. Jack had been made to feel like a villain for taking the job, but then he met Harry, another tree surgeon hired by Caldwell, who said that as far as he was concerned, the loss of healthy trees was the only downside in a long list of positives.

Jack had gone through a dark patch since moving to middle-of-nowhere Hesket, away from the liveliness of the city and people his own age. The gloomies, as Oonagh used to call it, had plagued Jack on and off since teenhood, flaring again when his granny had become ill and worsening progressively. It had been difficult, some days, to get out of bed; the isolation, the joylessness, was overwhelming. But then he'd met Harry, and gradually the murk lifted, and he was both grateful and relieved for it. Harry was switched on to the world in a way that Jack had never been. He planned to go to university and get a degree in political science (he was saving for it now) and talked impassionedly about his interest in social change and activism. It was his enthusiasm that Jack admired, his proclivity for thinking of what would benefit the whole rather than the individual, which inspired Jack to see the development as more than just money in his own pocket.

'It's tricky,' Jack was saying one day, 'because I don't have anything against Caldwell or the development. They're paying me a decent wage.' The two of them had been dragging branches to the Banshee, which was what they called the chipper truck on account of the horrendous screeching noise it made while obliterating anything unfortunate enough to be fed into it. 'But my grandpa's fuming. He says it's unconscionable.' And then, in imitation, *'Don't those idiots know about climate change?'*

'That's a tough one, mate.' Harry shook his head sympathetically. 'I'd hate it if my family disagreed with the way I make a living. I don't envy you.'

'He has a point, though.' They'd reached the Banshee, and Jack had to raise his voice over the rumbling motor. 'I get it.'

'Look, I don't want to lose any of our countryside either, but it's a needs-must situation.' Harry lugged the severed end of his branch into the chipper, guiding it towards the funnelled mouth. 'No offence to your grandpa, but the village is full of old people. To keep smaller communities going you need to bring in young folk, families. Increasing population size in rural areas is a positive.' The Banshee gripped the branch then, began devouring it savagely. He looked back at Jack, perhaps to make sure he could be heard over the piercing noise of the machine, and shouted, 'People around here need to understand that it's not just about building houses; it's regenerating the community. All this fearmongering is just the village cutting off their nose to spite their face.'

'Careful,' Jack warned. 'Watch your hands.' It was only a moment that Harry took his eye off the chipper, but a moment is enough for everything to change.

Harry must have thought that Jack meant he was closer to the blades than he actually was, because he'd startled then, flinching away abruptly, and in doing so lost his balance and fell precariously forward onto the branch as it was being fed into the machine, so that he was surfing it towards the mulching mechanism, to certain death, the branch pulling Harry in too quickly for Jack to shut the machine down, to react in any way other than grabbing him by the wrist and wrenching it back, a movement that twisted his arm behind and up, dislocating his shoulder, so Jack had to drive him to the nearest hospital.

It was not the only incident the site had seen; in fact, the more trees they'd cleared, the more things had gone wrong. Most disturbing were the freak accidents that left tree surgeons with years of experience seriously injured. There'd been an unusually high number of trees splitting as they were being felled and then falling in unexpected directions, almost crushing people who'd been properly stood well out of the danger zone. One man's chainsaw had kicked back and lacerated his neck, and he'd very nearly bled out and died. Someone else had broken their back when the branch anchoring their rope somehow tore away from the trunk, so that the lowering rope, climbing rope and tree surgeon were pulled with the branch as it fell to the ground. And there were so many more near misses that people began to wonder if the whole operation wasn't jinxed. Superstition caught like a wildfire, and there was a general consensus among the team that the woods themselves felt sinister, as if they pulsed with a strange energy, and this gave rise to jokes about it being haunted, though Jack did not remember them having ever felt creepy when he was a boy, did not necessarily think they felt so now. The unease only intensified when one of the woodland's oldest oaks was discovered to have the words *deth be not the ende here* cut crudely into its crooked trunk, half-hidden beneath a thatch of moss; the carving was misshapen and shallowed where the tree had widened and the bark thickened over centuries, and deeper into the woods, yet more trees were still faintly scarred with strange geometric shapes, like daisies in a wheel. A number of people had already quit by the time the site was temporarily shut down due to health and safety.

'Do you think it'll get reopened?' Jack said, when he'd met Harry for a pint at the pub.

'I don't see why not.' Harry shrugged. 'They're not gonna find anything. The site isn't in breach of the regulations, it's just been unlucky.'

'My grandpa's pretty stoked.' Jack had a swig of his beer. 'He's hoping it stays closed.'

'Then maybe you should inform him about rural demographics. Like I said earlier, cities are getting younger, towns and villages are getting older, so what happens to a place when there's no one left to live in it? If he loves Hesket, then the development is the only way to save it before it dies.'

After nearly an hour working away at clearing the tree, with rain so fine that it clung to him, he could smell the damp cotton of his T-shirt and the faint metallic tang of his own sweat as heat radiated from under his collar. Walter appeared, wearing Oonagh's polka-dotted plastic raincoat, tight across his stomach and short in the sleeves, so that a good two inches or so of his thick, hairy wrists were showing.

Walter handed him his own jacket, the proper waxed kind (apparently Jack could not be trusted with Oonagh's things now), and without a word began moving some of the smaller branches onto a pile. This was not, Jack knew, forgiveness, but rather his grandpa's uncompromising need to make himself useful.

Even though Jack had already been out in the mizzle too long for the coat to do much good, he put it on anyway. As he tugged it over his shoulders, he caught the faint scent of Walter's cologne, lemony and clean. He'd known that smell his entire life, and it provoked in him a sense of nostalgic ease, tender memories of languid childhood summer holidays and years of cosy, boisterous Christmases, which was why it shocked him to realise Walter no longer smelled this way, that at some point after Oonagh's passing, he'd stopped wearing it. A sudden and profound sadness overcame Jack then, the intensity of it so astonishing that he felt the need to turn away and look up at the sky behind him, to let it pass unnoticed by Walter. As he stood there, waiting for his eyes to clear, he knew that his grandpa was watching him because he could no longer hear the vinyl swish of Oonagh's plastic jacket as Walter piled chopped wood. It was obvious what Jack was doing, surely, but Walter said nothing. His grandpa found things like this – sentimentalities, displays of emotion – unbearable from a man in a way that he did not from a woman; Oonagh had said it was a hangover from his generation, when men did not talk about things like feelings or what was troubling their mind, believing that it was better to leave such things unspoken, but then their son – Jack's dad – had never been much good at it either, and consequently, neither was Jack, and the whole thing was passed from father to son like an inheritance. When at last Jack turned round again, Walter, as if compelled by some chain reaction, continued with his task as though he hadn't stopped at all, gathering and piling, and looking only at the wood in his hands.

Overhead, the rain gradually cleared, as the dark, woollen clouds travelled onward to other parts of Norfolk to release themselves fully.

When Jack finally set to digging up the stump, he didn't expect to find tangled there, in its latticework of roots, so many pieces of bone. Things had been unearthed in his grandparents' garden before – old tools, cloudy jewel-coloured bottles of many shapes, bits of pottery, a granite plinth in what was now the flower bed and given new life as a nightstand – and so at first he'd assumed the same again, that the row of flat, prong-like fragments caught within the matting of clod and root was just another crumbling garden fork. Jack pushed at the stump, rocking it like a loose molar so that there came the dull snap of root and hiss of falling dry soil onto the metal spade wedged beneath, and then came a thud of something larger hitting it – the old garden fork, he'd presumed – and as he stooped to retrieve it, he realised instead that he was looking at a segment of ribcage, that the gnarled knots of wood below were vertebrae, and he saw then the profile of a jaw lodged near the bottom right with its incomplete row of teeth, and above that, the partial rounding of a skull, a portion of its eye socket visible and plugged with earth, and he shouted then, hands leaping reflexively from the stump like a startled cat as he shunted it away sharply, the root ball thrusting upward a little higher so that the bones lifted with it and seemed to judder alive and find one another, as if clambering from the ground to meet him.

'Shitting hell!'

'What?' Walter said, from where he was clearing fallen leaves at the top of the garden.

Jack swore again, louder.

'Did you find a slow worm?' Walter put down the rake and walked over. 'Because it's not a snake, you know. It's just a lizard without legs.'

'No,' Jack said. 'I don't know. It's human. Bones.'

Walter peered into the hole. 'Gordon Bennett,' he said. 'How long do you think those have been there?'

'There's a skull.'

Walter tutted impatiently. 'I can see that.'

Jack pulled his phone from his pocket. 'We should call the police.'

'No.' Walter dismissed the idea immediately, waving it away with his hands. 'No way.'

'What?' Jack cried. 'Why?'

'The garden's been through enough today.'

'Are you joking?' Jack said. 'We have to tell someone. We can't just ignore remains.'

'It's *my* house and therefore *my* decision, and I said no. Your poor granny, all the work she put into this garden; I'm not having some bozos come in and ruin it even more, turn her home into a crime scene, dig everything up like they do on TV. And for what? Some mouldy old bones we didn't even know were there a minute ago? Out of the question.' He turned to Jack then, jabbed his finger at the air between them. 'You've done more than enough damage already.' And then he spun round and marched back inside the house, shutting the door forcefully behind him.

It stunned Jack, just how contrary, how unreasonable, his grandpa's outburst was; the bones should be the priority, anyone rational would agree. But clearly, Walter was still too set in his anger, and so Jack took a deep breath, tried to understand this apparent indifference to the discovery at his feet. Looking at them, the bones were undoubtedly very old, had been underground so long that they'd taken on a patina similar to the soil around them, more brown than pale. They must at least be as old as the tree that had grown on top of them, which was, itself, centuries in age; Jack had found the growth rings so numerous and so concentrated that in places one faint line could not be distinguished from another. All the police's efforts, then – all that destruction Walter was afraid of – would likely be for nought but acquiring remains the police could do nothing with, and since they were so much older than anyone in living memory it was unlikely they'd warrant an investigation, and would probably sit forgotten in a bag on a dusty storage shelf until someone eventually, pitilessly, got rid of them. And so the longer he stood there, the more Jack understood that he would not tell anyone, not yet; things were difficult enough with his grandpa at the moment, what with all that had passed between them, and the skeleton would have to wait. It was disturbing and macabre, but it was not, he supposed, urgent. He would give it a little while, let his grandpa calm down at least, and then he would call the police whether Walter approved or not.

For posterity, because it was the most interesting thing he'd found – would ever find – he took a picture of it with his phone, before replacing the stump and loosely filling in the dirt again (there was no point in doing it well, he thought, if he was only going to have to dig it up again to show the police).

The rest of the day passed much less eventfully, with evening falling quickly, and the two of them settling in for dinner and a round of television, and all the while Jack could not stop thinking about the skeleton in the garden, out there in the dark with its soil-packed eye sockets and naked teeth, and wondering who it once was and why they'd been buried there instead of in the nearby churchyard. If Walter was similarly preoccupied, he hid it well, and fell asleep in his chair, snoring lightly, until Jack woke him when it was finally late enough to go up to bed.

Jack's room overlooked the garden, and he stood at the window with the lights off so that he could see the stump in the moonlight. From this height, the top of it looked like an eye peering from behind a spy glass, with its blackened rotten centre surrounded by healthy wood. He imagined that it was the skeleton's eye, and he stared at it for a long time, half-expecting it to blink, for the eye to rove around and drink everything in, and he unnerved himself by remembering the way the bones had shifted as he'd disturbed the roots, how it felt to him now, that for a wild instant the skeleton had been alive, reaching for him, like it wanted to pull him down into its grave. And then, as if he'd commanded it, he saw the stump move, a slight pitch forward so that its eye was peering towards him, as if it knew he was there and wanted to look right back at him, and his heart begin to kickdrum, and the skin on the back of his neck contracted and—

Had it actually changed position, though? Almost certainly it was just an optical illusion, a shifting of the clouds filtering the moon's glow in a different way, and he blinked hard, refocusing, waiting for it to stir again, to reveal itself as something other than a trick of his overactive imagination, but after several long minutes the adrenalin began to subside, and he rationalised himself out of whatever it was he thought he'd seen as nothing but his own tired mind playing against him, and then climbed into bed before he could will the dead to life a second time.

The following day, the entire village gathered at the little church up the road to discuss the plight of Spry Wood. Because Walter was worried that his grandson's absence might make people talk, Jack agreed – albeit reluctantly – to attend, and now his afternoon was to be spent sat on an uncomfortable rigid pew surrounded by people who would hate him if they ever found out what he'd been doing. They were sat near Nell, who'd behaved oddly since his granny's memorial. When Oonagh passed, Jack, wanting to spare Walter the pain of informing all her friends and acquaintances of her passing, had volunteered to go through her address book himself. He'd called the first name he came to in its alphabetised pages: Judy Bennett, who insisted that *she* take on the task instead, because she knew *exactly* who should be told, and Jack, grateful that he wouldn't have to repeat the same painful conversation, let her. It didn't occur to him that there should be a hierarchy of respect, as Walter put it later, that Nell should have been called first. It had caused confusion and upset, and now she would hardly look at him.

The church continued to fill with people – Jack knew many of them from the village or from the few occasions he'd helped Walter at the allotment, and there were people he'd never seen before too, who must have come from the neighbouring hamlets.

Emir, one of his grandpa's allotment friends, took the empty space beside Jack. He had short curly hair and was softly spoken, and began talking to Walter about his crop being nearly ready to pick, any day now really, and Walter shared all the ways in which he was still using up runner beans from the freezer after his glut in July – in casseroles and stews, on their own with a bit of salt and garlic; have you tried making them into chutney, Emir asked, because he has a recipe . . .

Jack, who was sat slouching between them but wanted no part of the conversation, wished that he hadn't had to come and was instead outside alone somewhere, smoking a cigarette, but too many people were seated in his pew now, and there was no room to squeeze past without everyone having to slide out and let him. The church was draughty and the pews hard, and there was a musty smell, like old, damp paper. He felt suddenly confined, in this place he didn't want to be, with these people he didn't really know, about to listen to more things he didn't want to listen to, things that were against the development and therefore against his job, which was in some way, then, against himself, and it was this sense of confinement that made him think of the skeleton wedged beneath the tree, and his silly imaginings the night before. Not that the skeleton had been far from his mind since yesterday. A back garden was not the right kind of resting place, and if there were such a thing as a soul, surely it would be unhappy about being there, in an unmarked grave. There'd been no coffin after all, and it didn't seem like one had simply rotted away, because the skeleton wasn't lying on its back, but was instead on its side with its leg bones tucked towards its skull, as if it had been dumped carelessly in the ground, which made it unlikely that it'd been buried by loved ones, and that was suggestive, wasn't it, of something wicked having happened to this person, something criminal? And underlying it all was the plain fact that there were now remains – human remains! – in the garden, the bones of someone, having lain near his bare boyhood feet as he played in the grass, hiding down there his whole life, and that thought alone was an unsettling one. While all of this swam about his head, he scrutinised the picture he'd taken on his phone, careful to hold it low by his lap out of the eye-line of anyone else, and as he examined the skeleton, which had once been a person of muscle and sinew and skin, he could imagine the parts rebuilding, joining into something whole . . .

'Are those bones?'

Emir was no longer speaking to Walter, but to him.

'Sorry,' Emir said. 'I didn't mean to be nosy, but.' He gestured to the picture on Jack's phone.

Walter looked sharply at Jack. 'Have I told you that Jack's moved in with me for a while?' He was trying to change the subject, that much was obvious. 'He's been very helpful around the house.'

'Did *you* find them?' Emir said. 'The bones?'

'Surely not,' Walter insisted.

Jack did not need the prod from Walter's elbow to know that he should deny having discovered them. 'A friend of mind did, over in Thetford.' And then, because he knew there would be more questions after so tantalisingly noncommittal an answer, 'Under a tree. He said they're old, hundreds of years probably, so there's no cause for concern.'

But what he'd hoped would end the conversation only seemed to excite Emir further. 'Oh wow, I've heard about this kind of thing,' he said loudly. 'I'm a bit of an amateur archaeologist; at least I would be if I wasn't a teacher.' People sitting nearby were glancing at them. 'There was a Norfolk practice back in the day called *harrowing a witch*.'

He paused, continuing again when no one said anything.

'Granted, it's an odd term, but the land was mostly used for agricultural farming then, including, probably, the meadow here in Hesket, so I imagine the name was derived from that; a harrow, as you might know, is a big tool with spiky teeth that's drawn over soil to remove weeds and bury seed.'

'I'm aware of what a harrow is,' Walter said, gesturing for Emir to keep his voice down.

Emir leaned in closer. 'Well, after executing a suspected witch, they'd plant a tree on top of the body because people were afraid she might rise again to exact her revenge. The idea was the witch would be imprisoned under the weight of the tree for as long as it stood.'

'Is that right?' Walter said distractedly.

Emir nodded. 'Afraid so. They'd even bury animals they thought were witches' familiars – hares, cats, that kind of thing. I'm teaching a unit on local history, and the witch trials are an interesting part of it. Obviously, we can't say for sure that's what this is.' He pointed at Jack's phone. 'I mean, we don't even know when these bones are dated, but it makes sense, given the area. Matthew Hopkins was pretty prolific around East Anglia, and there were even women accused here in Hesket. In fact, the trees that would've been used locally for harrowing are probably still standing today, though maybe not for much longer, given what's going on here.'

Jack nodded politely. 'I'll tell my friend. Thanks.'

'Is he an archaeologist?'

'Tree surgeon.'

'He should really get in touch with a museum in case the bones are significant. What did the authorities say?'

'Jack's a tree surgeon too,' Walter said quickly. 'This is just an acquaintance from work.' And then, to Jack, 'That's why he sent you the picture, isn't it? For work.'

'Is that right?' Emir said. 'What do you think about cutting down Spry Wood then?'

'He thinks it's outrageous,' Walter said, 'same as everyone else.'

'Yeah,' Jack lied. 'Horrible.'

A hush descended as the vicar, Rev. Eileen Wright, gestured for everyone's attention, and Jack was thankful to put his phone away. He'd only met Eileen a handful of times but found her to be confident and charismatic, and because these were qualities which reminded him of his grandmother, he sat up and listened to her.

'Thank you all for coming,' she said. 'As you must be aware, this meeting has been called in light of the recent hiatus at the development site. I thought it might be a good idea for us to regroup as a community and—' She cleared her throat. 'I've invited a representative from Caldwell to attend so that we have the opportunity to voice our concerns directly.' It was then that Jack noticed the short woman standing near Eileen. 'Let's all welcome Patricia Wilson, who has kindly agreed to join us today.'

Patricia smiled at the attendees before her, as dulcet tones of murmuring filled the church.

'This is an open discussion,' Eileen continued, 'so any thoughts or ideas are welcome.'

'Any at all,' Patricia agreed.

It was Paul who worked at the retirement home that spoke first. 'Well, clearly the whole operation's bloody dangerous.' He was sat between his sons, Hardy and Finn. 'Or you wouldn't have had to shut it down. That's my thought.'

There were noises of agreement.

Patricia looked unfazed by the immediacy with which the condemnation had begun. 'I can assure you—'

'I feel that someone has died on site but it's being kept

quiet.' It was Celia who chimed in now, the odd woman who always wore shawls (*Every village has at least one eccentric,* Oonagh had said of her). 'It's probably why Health and Safety got involved.'

'That's simply not true,' Patricia said calmly. 'There have been no fatalities on site whatsoever.'

'Only injuries,' Eileen said. 'Though you have to admit, there's been a lot of them.'

'It's the curse of Old Hesket,' Nell blurted.

A young woman who Jack didn't recognise turned right around in her seat to look at Nell.

'Forgive me, Vicar, I know this probably isn't the most appropriate setting to say that word,' Nell said, gesturing to the rafters above. 'But all those injuries don't just happen for no reason.'

More murmuring, interspersed now with chuckling; Nell looked steadfastly at the front of the room, her cheeks beginning to pink.

'If I may.' Patricia held up her hands, imploring them to silence. 'I'm not familiar with the . . .' She seemed to consider the right way to respond. 'The *nuances* of your village. But it's clear that safety is a concern for you all, and I completely agree with you. It *should* be a concern. *We're* very concerned that there have been *any* injuries at all. We're as shocked as you are. But we're also aware that it doesn't do any good to dwell in a climate of fear. I can assure you that site safety protocols have been rigorously followed from the beginning, so it makes no sense to us why these accidents have occurred, but we are working closely with the Health and

Safety Executive to make sure it doesn't happen again. It's in our best interest to ensure the welfare of our team.'

'And what about the best interest of the woodland?' Daniel from next door said. 'Why isn't that being thought of? It's bad enough climate change is messing with the natural seasons and making our trees lose their leaves prematurely, but now you lot want to kill them off entirely?'

'Exactly,' Walter said. 'What about all those poor old trees that have been there for hundreds, maybe even thousands, of years? What about respecting Mother Nature?'

Patricia was nodding diplomatically. 'I completely understand. The world needs more trees, not fewer, which is why we've pledged to plant one hundred saplings across Norfolk through our tree planting initiative. And I want to stress that we're keeping a large part of Spry Wood intact, which you'll be free to continue to enjoy. All trees with bat roosts on the site will be saved as well, which is why we've employed skilled tree surgeons capable of more delicate work instead of bulldozers. We take climate and environmental challenges very seriously. We also take communities seriously, which is why we're committed to helping young people get on the housing ladder. Half the homes we build in Hesket will be affordable for first-time buyers and suitable for growing families.'

This must have impressed some people in the audience, because a few of them began making quiet sounds of approval.

'The long-term plan is to introduce a small number of retail spaces – a café, a greengrocer – conveniences that will provide jobs and boost the local economy. We'll also be building a golf course, and we're going to offer anyone in the community over the age of sixty a discounted membership.'

More agreeable noises.

The discussion continued like this for the better part of an hour. When at last the meeting was over and they were all making their way outside, Jack saw the woman who'd turned around earlier approaching them.

'Excuse me, Ms Riley, is it?' she said. 'My name is Rio and I'm with the *Norfolk Times*. You said something very interesting during the discussion tonight, and I'd love to hear more about it, if you wouldn't mind speaking to me?'

'*Me?* Saying *interesting* things?' Nell said, so that everyone else could hear. 'I'd be delighted to speak with you.'

Walter and Jack left her to it, walking in silence through the churchyard and out into the road, where the people not from Hesket were getting into their cars.

'Well?' Walter said when they were alone. 'What did you think about that?' As if Jack now had reason to change his mind, to think twice about returning to work for a company that was clearly so vile. In truth, Jack thought the meeting accomplished the opposite of what was intended of it; rather than maligning the development entirely, the attendees, at least a small portion of them, seemed to have woken up to the good it could do.

'I think Granny would be worried Nell was losing her marbles.'

'Mmm,' Walter said, pushing open the gate in front of his house and walking up the path.

'Emir said some interesting things,' Jack said, 'about the bones.'

'If you say so.' Walter took out his keys, unlocked the door.

Jack followed him inside. 'You don't agree?'

Walter shrugged off his jacket and hung it up. As he walked into the living room, he said, 'Interesting is hardly the word I'd use. Dull, more like.' He turned on the television and sat in his chair, began flicking through channels.

'I meant it's interesting to think about,' Jack said from the hallway. 'It could be why there's someone buried in the garden.'

'I'd rather not, if you don't mind,' he said, turning up the volume. '*Pointless* is on.'

When Jack ventured downstairs the next morning, rolling a cigarette, he found Walter in the kitchen with a broom in his hand.

'I was wondering when you were going to get up,' Walter said.

Jack frowned, palmed his hair, which was messy from sleep. 'What time is it?'

'I found an absolute tip downstairs this morning.' Walter gestured with widened arms as if to show him, but the kitchen looked just the same as it had before; there were old coffee stains on the counter, a scattering of spilled porridge oats still on the floor near the oven.

'I've cleaned it up now, but the back door was wide open when I came down. There was soil all over the place, and bits of the garden blown in everywhere. I think we had a visitor, too; I thought maybe an animal because the kitchen was a right state, all the cupboards and fridge open, things strewn about—'

'The fridge?' Jack said. 'What kind of an animal was opening the fridge?'

'Well,' Walter said, 'that's the thing. You aren't going to believe me when I tell you.'

'Go on then.'

Walter took something out of his pocket, and set it triumphantly down on the counter, looking at Jack as if to say, *Ta-da!*

The object was small, about half the length of his thumb, and pale brown, like an old stick.

'I found it by my pillow this morning,' Walter said.

Jack tucked the cigarette behind his ear, aware that his grandpa was watching him closely, waiting for a reaction in the same way he used to when playing a trick. *He we go again*, Oonagh used to sigh. *He's got that glint about his eye.* Two years ago, Jack had taken refuge in the spare room (the very room he occupied now) following the breakdown of a relationship; it was his first and devastating, and he'd been booted unceremoniously out of the rental he'd moved into with his ex only months before. Oonagh had emptied his binbags of their scant possessions and arranged them in the room so that it felt less temporary while he looked for a new flat, because a broken heart was bad enough without feeling like you didn't have a home as well. With Oonagh, he drank his weight in tea as she encouraged him to talk about what had happened in fine detail, persuaded him out of sending any kind of desperate, pleading texts, and she hugged him, spontaneously and often, rubbing circles into his back the way she used to when he was a boy. Walter was not involved in these particular conversations, had a knack of disappearing from the room altogether when they began. Instead, he pretended for the better part of a week that he'd bumped his head and turned French. He reprogrammed the TV in French, ate only baguettes and French cheeses when Jack was around, and spoke in French (though this hadn't lasted long because his grasp of the language was limited to a few tourist-centric phrases learned on holiday, so he resorted to French-accented English, influenced heavily by Inspector Clouseau). It had been altogether baffling behaviour until Oonagh said, *But aren't you just lighter when he's around? Who knew the French would be so good at making us forget our troubles?* And it was true.

Since his granny's death, his grandpa had remained an enigma to Jack, only now there was no one to explain to him why Walter was excited about a bit of wood.

Jack picked it up; it was not, as he'd thought, a stick. 'It looks porous,' he said. 'What is it?' But he knew what it was, knew it as soon as he'd asked the question.

'I had the most vivid dream about your grandmother last night,' Walter said excitedly. 'She was in my room. I saw her standing at the foot of the bed. You know how sometimes when a dream feels so real you think you're awake?'

'This is bone,' Jack said. Instinctively, he glanced out the window, out towards the skeleton.

'Do you see what I'm saying? She must know how much

I—' Walter's voice suddenly failed him then, catching both him and Jack by surprise. He cleared his throat loudly, perhaps in an effort to rid it of the emotion that had ambushed him, and seemed unable to bring himself to look at Jack, who in that moment was fearful – felt a genuine alarm – that it would overcome Walter and Jack would see him cry, yet at the same time, he wanted his grandpa to allow it to come rather than push it down, wanted so badly for them to finally be the kind of men who could hold one another, who could comfort the way Oonagh had.

Walter continued, almost pleadingly. 'You know how she was always finding things, always collecting. This house is filled with little bits just like that, bones and such. I don't believe it's a coincidence that I dream she's in the room with me and then wake up to that on my bed. She was there, I'm telling you, *really* there.' He sighed, looking at Jack again. 'You think I'm daft.'

It was not beyond reason that there should be a piece of bone in the house. Oonagh brought home a dead kingfisher and had it stuffed after all, and Jack remembered her once boiling the tiny skull of a shrew so that she could display it.

Walter was still holding the broom in his hand, and Jack took it from him gently, leaning it against the counter. 'What about the kitchen, then? You said the door was open.'

'I suppose it was her way of letting us know she isn't happy about her favourite tree being cut down,' he said. 'By making a tip of things.'

'Granny hated a mess, though.'

'Exactly,' Walter said, as if this proved his point.

Jack thought of the keys in the bathroom cabinet, the hob left on all day. He knew how temperamental the latch on that door was if they forgot to lock it, how easily it could have blown open in the night.

'Well, I'm glad,' Jack said. 'If you feel good about it, then I'm glad.'

Walter gestured out the window. 'I think something's burrowed underneath the stump. See how it's sunk where the soil's shifted? Maybe a rabbit or a badger.'

The stump most definitely sat on a wonk; there was no trick of the imagination now.

The morning was clear, with a pale disc faintly etched above the stump in that ever-changing sky; the same moon that had always been. 'It's nice you're here,' Walter said quietly. 'I've been meaning to tell you that.' Neither of them looked at the other. It seemed then that an invisible presence had enveloped them, a feeling long-gone, returned now, familiar and reassuring, a remainder of the past that would surely dissipate like a haze when at last one of them moved or spoke, unreachable again.

For the rest of the day there was something Jack couldn't shake. Despite his reasoning, it bored away in the dark of his mind, like a worm in old wood. He examined the piece of bone against the photo on his phone; remarkable, how similar the colour was, how all bone left in the ground, then, must take on the same patina. But that little worm didn't let it alone, and insisted that he trace back what he knew:

The back door open all night.

The bone on the pillow.

The burial beneath the heft of a tree so the dead don't rise.

And the tree all but gone, nothing but a small stump there now, hardly any weight at all.

Finn

On nights the moon was round and brilliant, and the sky yawned silver-blue and cloudless, Daddo led them across the hay meadow by torch light, navigating hollowed wells of animal burrows and clumsy knots of tussock grass. Daddo said the best time for fishing was at night under a bright moon, because fish have the double misfortune of being allergic to the sun and half-blind.

'That's how come you see little bubbles on the surface sometimes,' he said. 'It's the fish sneezing.'

Even Hardy fell for that one.

Over time, Finn had come to realise that the real reason they went out in the dark was because Daddo wanted to keep whatever they caught for the frying pan instead of letting it back into the river like they were supposed to. If the biting was good, they'd land bream or roach, or even a perch if luck was on their side, and cook the fish for breakfast with a squeeze of lemon; and if it wasn't, carp or tench, which tasted muddy even with a crusting of salt flakes and parsley. Daddo used to joke that angling was his mistress but stopped after the divorce, and started saying instead that it was his one true sweetheart. He'd named Hardy for the reel that caught him his first fish, and Finn for the fish, because it was more palatable than naming him Brown Trout. Hardy told Finn that that had been one of the reasons why their mum upped and moved to Beccles – because she hated their names so much – and for months, Finn believed him.

But then today Finn asked Daddo why they couldn't just have regular names, and the story about Mum was let slip, and Daddo grounded Hardy for lying. The two of them shouted at each other in a way Finn hadn't seen before, in a way that seemed to surprise Daddo, too. Hardy had plans with his friends, he said, and didn't think it was his fault that Finn was such a gullible baby, which only grounded him for longer, because Finn pretended it had hurt his feelings. Daddo went for a walk to cool off, and when he returned, he said that the night air made him better, so he decided that after dinner they were all going to get out and go fishing, even though they had school in the morning and the moon was only a waning crescent. They walked the meadow in silence by the light of Hardy's phone torch, listening out for anyone who might catch them with their fishing gear. They'd had a close call at the end of summer, a man out running across the meadow, shouting *Wait!* over and over again, *Please don't go!*, following them through the dark and into the woods, and they'd had to kill the light and hide behind a large clump of bracken, waiting with breath held until long after whoever it was had passed them by, panting hard and moaning, like sad ghosts do in the movies. *What kind of plonker goes for a run at night without any lights on him?* Daddo whispered.

When they reached the boundary of Spry Wood, they skirted the edge of the development site, following the tall chain-link fence that had recently been put up to keep everyone else out, a new safety precaution now that the felling of trees was in full swing again. The area they'd felled made it look as though a large bite of the woods was missing, and Finn imagined that a giant had wandered by in the night and eaten the trees, one by one, like florets of broccoli. Through the gap, Finn could see the river, a mysterious underworld, shifting and glinting in the dark, and he thought then, as he always did when looking on the river at night, of what Daddo said he'd seen there once, a monster with hungry eyes and rows of sharp, savage teeth, a beast so big he couldn't see its end in the water, and a way about it that seemed intelligent, cunning even. They made their way along the fence that cut the woods in two, the starkness of the development site on their left, untouched woods on their right, followed it all the way to the river. They settled finally at the old stone bridge where the moon shattered across the water, and aimed for pieces of it glinting in the slow current as they cast their lines out into the night. The best place to fish was here at Pelham's Lookout, though it wasn't really called that. Arthur Pelham was the man who lived in Hex Cottage overlooking the bridge (they discovered the name several months ago, after a hand-painted sign appeared on the gate). Because he lived in geographical isolation from the rest of the village, and because no one ever saw him leave the cottage, Hardy naturally had stories about him: that he had a cauldron in which he made potions or was really an eccentric millionaire who preferred the appearance of poverty, that he was in the witness protection programme.

The three of them sat quietly for a little while, with only the sounds of the trees shivering around them and the rustling of clawed animals in the undergrowth.

'Bats are out,' Daddo said. 'Over the river, look.'

Finn was not afraid of the shadows darting and swooping to disappear again into the trees. Instead, it was the way the clouds passed continually over the moon, plunging them into a deep, wide-open darkness that spooked him.

'I bet carp,' Hardy said, his voice cracking in that way it had lately started to. His reel clicked as he patiently inched in his line, hoping to tempt a bite. 'Maybe a roach. But tonight feels like carp.'

'Don't say that,' said Daddo. 'We've left that kind of talk at home.' Daddo was superstitious about manifesting undesirable fish; if it was said aloud, it would come true.

'Roach, then.'

'We'll get perch,' Finn said. 'Hardy'll get a carp.'

Perhaps because Hardy had already jinxed them and their luck was now irreversibly set, Daddo sighed and said, 'As long as none of us pull in an eel. Bland as shite.'

When they were younger, Hardy made up a game called The Eel King, which had them puffing out their cheeks and moving their arms slowly as if they were swimming underwater, even though they were standing in the living room.

It usually involved Finn being caught desperately between rocks – which were actually just sofa cushions – awaiting certain death at the jaws of a giant eel until Hardy came to his rescue, wrestling madly with the creature – the armchair – in order to save his little brother, before freeing Finn and swimming with him around the room until they finally reached his boat – the coffee table – and then the two of them would sail off in search of adventure together. Hardy was no longer interested in The Eel King because he was at secondary school.

'Their blood is toxic.' Hardy's reel clicked in the dark. 'Did you know?'

Finn tutted.

'It *is*,' said Hardy. 'That's why it's never served raw in sushi restaurants.'

'You've never been to a sushi restaurant.'

'Yeah I have.'

'Since when?'

'In Norwich.'

'With who?'

The question hung in the dark for a few stretched moments. From somewhere near, a lone owl called, stilling the scurry of rodents in the undergrowth.

'It's true.' Daddo cleared his throat. 'A tiny amount can stop a heart dead.'

Finn looked out at the river. 'Yeah right.'

'Captain,' Daddo said. 'The Captain' had been the name of their now-departed cat; to swear untruthfully on him was an offence that was simply not done.

Finn could hear the satisfaction in Hardy's voice when he said, 'Told you.'

'When did you go to Norwich?' Finn said. 'I want to go to Norwich.'

'Anyway.' Hardy cast his line out again, though there was too little light to tell with any certainty where it landed. 'I'm more worried about eels in the loo, to be honest with you. There's a man just last week who got bitten on the arse by one when he went for a poo in the night. It was in the news.'

Finn snorted. 'No there wasn't.'

'Honest. You know those sewage outflows that empty into rivers and stuff? Apparently that's how they get into the plumbing; it all connects to each other. Think about it.'

The trouble was that it sort of made sense.

As casually as he could, Finn said, 'So what happened to him, then?'

Hardy and Daddo each began to draw their lines in, reels clicking unhurriedly and out of time.

'Obviously he had to go to hospital. I mean, he's fine *now*. But that's the kind of thing that stays with a person. Every time he uses a toilet, he'll be crapping himself.'

Daddo must have appreciated the joke because he laughed quietly, which Finn knew Hardy would've *loved*. He thought about all those times he'd used the loo in the middle of the night and hadn't even so much as glanced into the bowl to know if there'd been an eel staring up at him, ready to sink in its needled teeth. 'You're making it up,' Finn said. 'You always make things up.'

Finn wasn't a storyteller, not like Hardy, who could pluck

one from anything. He got it from Daddo, who told stories to calm them before bed when they were little, to entertain them if the TV got cut off when he was out of work. There was the time, years ago, that Hardy said the trees in a wood swapped places with each other at night to confuse people, and Finn still liked to imagine it was true. There were the stories about how clouds didn't actually move across the sky, that it was an illusion caused by the earth rotating beneath them, or how colour didn't exist in the past, which was why the photograph of their great-gran was black and white, that inhaling enough helium from birthday balloons could make a person float, and that Finn's favourite teacher, Ms Pekter, lived at school with all the other teachers, how islands and continents only floated on the surface and you could swim beneath them, the seeds in strawberries were really fly eggs, and that flicking the lights on and off fast enough would make the switch catch fire.

And then Hardy said, 'That's not even the scariest thing, though.' He sighed heavily, as if what he were about to say pained him. 'You remember Dean Sankar, from school?'

'What about him?' Finn said.

'Well, that's the thing,' Hardy said. 'He was got by an *electric* eel.'

'What do you mean?'

'He went swimming here in summer and had a great big mark in the shape of a lightning bolt on his leg when they pulled him out, like a current had gone right through his body, and that was the end of him.'

'No,' Finn said. 'He moved away.'

'That's what the school wanted people to think because

they didn't want to scare anyone.' Hardy's line whooshed as he cast it out.

'That isn't true,' Finn said, looking at Daddo and then at Hardy. 'I know you're just being a Pretending Parker.' That was what Mum used to call Daddo, even though his name was Paul. She'd stopped Daddo from telling his frightening stories in front of Finn and Hardy, those stories that grown men tell, but she'd never forbade Hardy from doing it, hadn't needed to in those days.

Hardy continued, as if Finn hadn't said anything. 'I know because I heard a couple of the teachers talking about it.'

'There aren't electric eels here.'

'There aren't *supposed* to be, sure,' Daddo said then. 'But electric eels do live in freshwater rivers. As long as a man's arm, those buggers.'

'Exactly,' Hardy said. 'They were brought here to Hesket. And guess who it was that put them in the Wensum.'

Finn's throat felt like there was a plum stone in it.

'Pelham,' Hardy said quietly. 'The eels are to keep people away; he breeds them in his bathtub.'

Hex Cottage looked eerily like it was watching them then, the way its wonky windows stared out from beneath its crooked roof, unnerving in its silhouette and its looming silence. And the river, like an obscure and cavernous abyss waiting to swallow him up, filled with all kinds of monstrous things; in the dark, there were crocodiles and sharks and giant bone-crushing snakes waiting for one of them to fall in, there were Loch Ness monsters and krakens, and unknown things terrifying enough to frighten even Daddo, and now, electric eels. He didn't like the river at night, preferred it in the day when it was a different thing entirely, placid and benign, a place he'd skipped stones with his mum.

He was used to Hardy's stories, but this one felt different, threatening in a way they never had before. He looked to Daddo and saw that he was grinning, which was a strange thing to do in that moment, and then suddenly there were hard fingers jabbing at his ribs and Finn was screaming, loud and pitched enough to be embarrassing, as Hardy made a zapping noise and pretended to electrocute him.

He leapt up, didn't care if he snapped the rod when he flung it at his feet. 'That's not funny,' he shouted. 'I'm going home.' He hated that his voice wobbled, that his tears came so quickly.

Daddo must have realised how frightened Finn had been then, because he said, 'Enough now, Hardy.' And when Hardy didn't stop, he said sharply, '*Hardy.*' And then, softer, 'Sorry, Finn, mate. That wasn't on.'

'I'm leaving,' Finn said again. But in the dark anything could get him, and so he just stood there, wishing that he were older and braver than he was.

'We're all going together,' Daddo said, getting to his feet. 'Now, Hardy.'

'We haven't caught anything, though,' Hardy said. 'We've only been out an hour.' But he did as he was told.

They walked back in silence, Daddo's hand on Finn's shoulder. And as they crossed the meadow, Hardy said, 'Hey, Finn, guess what.'

'What,' he said sulkily.

Then Hardy made a farting noise with his mouth, so long and wet and ridiculous, that Finn couldn't help but to laugh at it, and the dark filled with the sound of them all, blowing raspberries and cackling the rest of the way home.

On Monday morning, Daddo was the last to come downstairs for breakfast. Hardy and Finn were at the table eating toast with jam, and Daddo popped two slices of bread in to brown for himself. It was the start of the half-term holiday, and Daddo had taken a couple of days off work so that they *didn't immediately go feral* in his absence.

'Right,' he said. He was wearing his robe and a towel round his shoulders, his hair wet. 'Who's been piddling in the shower?' He looked at each of them, drying his ears with a towelled finger.

Finn froze, aware of his skin beginning to bloom while Hardy laughed as if it was the funniest thing anyone had ever said.

'I'm serious,' said Daddo. 'I'm sick of standing in a puddle when I get in. Which one of you is it?'

'It's not *me*.' Hardy looked amused and horrified at the same time. 'I'm not an animal. Ask *him*.'

Daddo held up his finger, indicating that it was time Hardy close his gob. 'Finn,' he said. 'What's going on, mate?'

Finn lowered his head even more. 'It's in case there's eels,' he mumbled.

'What?' Daddo said.

'That can get in from the pipes,' Finn said. 'That can bite your arse.'

Hardy started laughing again, hysterical this time.

'You said it was in the paper,' Finn shouted at him. 'You said he had to go to hospital.'

'I can't believe you're *such* a child,' Hardy yelped.

'Hardy,' Daddo warned.

'It's not my fault he's pissin' in the bath.'

'*Hardy.*'

'Yeah, shut it, Hardy,' Finn said loudly.

The toast popped up.

'Enough, the both of you.' Daddo was rubbing his forehead. 'You,' he said to Finn, 'no more of this. You either use the toilet from now on or you hold it until morning. And you—' He turned to glare at Hardy. 'Stop being so bloody antagonistic.'

'Fine, I won't ever talk to him again.'

'Good.' Daddo retrieved his toast and last week's newspaper folded roughly on the counter. 'No one talk ever from now on.'

Hardy rolled his eyes, but took another slice of bread from the bag, glowering at Finn as he tore hunks from it and chewed.

Stop looking at me, Finn mouthed.

'Uh-uh.' Daddo did not glance up as he read the sports column. 'That's talking.'

Silence for a short while.

Hardy drummed his fingers on the table. He looked at the oven clock.

Daddo licked his finger and turned the page. 'Somewhere to be?'

'The guys want to go fishing.'

Daddo looked up at him, pleasantly surprised.

'They want to learn how.'

'That's great then,' Daddo said, quite happily. 'I'd planned on doing some work at the allotment today, but I suppose I could be persuaded to the river instead.' He was smiling. 'Maybe we could bust out the boat.' Daddo had recently saved up for a second-hand rowing boat, currently housed beneath a tarp in the garden, awaiting a re-oil and a new coat of paint.

'Actually,' Hardy said, 'I was just going to ask if I could take another rod? They don't have any.'

'Oh.' Daddo hesitated. 'Right.' He looked down at the paper once again and said in a voice that sounded both deflated and falsely cheerful, 'So long as you're careful with it then.'

Hardy's ears reddened. 'Thanks,' he mumbled. 'I'm going to take a shower so don't do any dishes.' He lingered at the table.

'Righto.' Daddo was staring intently at an advert for washing-up liquid.

'I want to go fishing,' Finn said.

'No,' Hardy said quickly. 'You can't come.'

'What about the allotment?' Daddo said. 'Just the two of us.'

Finn made a whining noise.

'So go fishing by yourself then,' Hardy said.

'But I won't catch anything by myself.'

Hardy was a better angler than Finn. This was partly because he had a height advantage, since he was by now nearly as tall as Daddo, which meant he could cast further, but also that he could see the choice spots he needed to aim for. Like Daddo, Hardy could read a river and its fish in a way that Finn could not, could get a measure of where the current slackened or broke or converged into a seam, and he knew how to find the fish in each of these places and what kind, could anticipate whether or not they'd bite. Daddo said that when Finn was tall enough to see it, he'd teach him, too.

'I don't care,' Hardy said. 'It's not my problem.'

'Give me strength.' Daddo sounded annoyed now. 'Stop bickering, the pair of you.' To Hardy, he said, 'I'm not having him stay here alone, melting his brain in front of that bleedin' tablet all day, watching God-knows-what. He wants to fish, so take him with you. End of.'

Hardy slammed his way past the table and out of the room, shouting about the injustice of it all. Daddo sighed and looked up at the ceiling, the way he tended to do when upset.

'Teenagers,' Finn said.

Daddo shrugged sadly. 'You'll be doing the same soon enough.' And it felt like a balloon filling too quickly in Finn's chest.

'No I won't.'

Daddo began to spread jam on his toast.

'I won't,' Finn said.

But Daddo only kissed Finn's head. 'Off with you then. In case he tries to go without you. And make sure he wears his jacket; it's chilly out.'

They walked in silence past the church and along the road where it rounded away from the village towards the river,

Hardy glued to his phone the whole time. Finn wondered why they were going this way, which was longer, instead of leaving through the back garden and cutting across the meadow. It became clear when they'd reached the place where the wood met the road that Hardy hadn't wanted Daddo to see them from the house, because he turned abruptly to Finn as they entered the treeline. 'You're not coming with me.'

'But Dad—'

'I'm not taking my little brother.' The words seemed to disgust him. 'You can stay here or go home or do whatever you want. But just don't follow me.'

'But what about these?' Finn held up the food waste bag that Daddo had filled with peanut butter and jam sandwiches; thick globs of purple clung to the inside of it.

'I don't care, you have them.'

'But there's too many,' Finn protested. 'He made enough for everyone.'

'Fine.' Hardy snatched the bag and practically threw one of the sandwiches back. 'There. Bye.'

'But why can't I just come?'

'Because it's *embarrassing*.'

It was said quickly and without thought. Guilt, or something like it, flashed briefly across Hardy's face and he wavered. 'You're so annoying,' he said, quietly exasperated, before turning and marching on without him.

Finn watched him leave, leaden with hurt. It occurred to him that he could probably do as Hardy suggested and go fishing by himself. Daddo had shown him how to lift the line out of the water in the right way, so that it didn't make a loud suction-cup *pop!* which would scare the fish. He'd taught him to bend from his elbow and not his wrist, and that when he lifted the line up and back, he should hold the rod by his ear and pause, like he was talking on the phone; that all the power should come from that backwards motion and not the forward cast, or else the line would drop in heavy tailing loops instead of whip-straight and far in front of him. But then, he didn't know how to map the river, couldn't see where it was that the fish should be, and even if he were by sheer chance to catch anything on his own, Hardy wouldn't be there with the net to help him pull it from the water, and the thought of removing the hook from its bloodied mouth by himself, and then having to lie precariously on his stomach, with his arms in the river to hold the fish upstream until it was strong enough to swim away again, filled him with panic; he had never done those things without Hardy or Daddo to oversee. He could find Daddo and say he'd changed his mind, but then there would be questions about Hardy and Finn might cry, and anyway, he didn't want to spend the day with the weirdos at the allotment, who genuinely found vegetables interesting.

He'd never been left in the woods all alone before, never noticed the deep, unnerving kind of stillness it had, as if the trees were collectively holding their breath, waiting for something to happen. His skin prickled with an awful kind of anticipation, the same as it did when the floorboard outside his bedroom door creaked if Hardy was there, skulking, before charging in and making Finn jump. The woods felt that way now, as if there was some other lurking presence seeping up from all around, alive in some way and aware of him standing there, something beyond himself or his brother, or the faraway sounds of men felling trees near the river, and he decided he would follow Hardy instead of spending the day unnervingly by himself, that at least it was company of a sort. He could pretend he was a spy and Hardy his target, a game they used to play before Hardy stopped being fun. He folded his sandwich in half and tucked it into his jacket pocket, moved as quietly and hurriedly as he could, avoiding anything that might crunch or snap, which was tricky, since everything was so dry. Now and then he'd duck quickly behind a tree or a withered clump of bracken, and peer out from behind them with his sandwich raised high like a pistol, scanning the trees ahead to keep Hardy in his sight while the wind muttered though countless branches, tugging free leaves in reds and golds that drifted lazily from the canopy like spring blossom.

At one point, Hardy veered sharply to the left, and as Finn trailed after him, the distant, inarticulate noise of voices and equipment grew louder as they reached the outskirts of the area that was being cleared. Hardy stood near the chain-link fence bisecting the woods and looked out at what had once been a grove of trees – oak, ash, beech, chestnut, silver birch, they'd named them all using an app on Daddo's phone, had even come each spring when the air smelled of the wild garlic that grew in abundance, and picked from its carpet of leaves for their dinner. Hardy remained there, perhaps thinking of wild garlic, too, and how those days would be gone now, until there came the loud crack of a falling branch like a shout, and he walked onward again. Finn approached the fence when the coast was clear; he'd not been down to the development site in the daytime before. There was a large machine that glared in the sun, brightly yellow and at odds with the landscape around it, and all over the ground was sawdust and raw holes where great big trees had been removed like teeth. It looked so desolate, so wrong. There was a man standing high up in a nearby oak with a rope from his waist looped around the trunk. He'd removed the canopy so there was nothing but a few radial stumps where its mighty branches should have been. The man killed the power on his chainsaw and clipped it to his utility belt, before letting it hang down the side of his leg. He lifted his visor and began to roll a cigarette as the men below dragged away the severed branches, and Finn recognised him at once as Mr Moody's grandson, Jack, and because he knew Daddo would think him a traitor, Finn raised his jammy sandwich to him and whispered, *Pow!*

He continued after Hardy for some time, not really conscious of the direction they were going in until he heard voices and realised he was approaching Pelham's Lookout. He snuck towards the sound, crouching awkwardly as he walked in order to keep hidden. Hardy was in the dip beside the bridge, not with his goon friends, but with a girl. She was the older sister of another boy in his class at the junior school, and had stuck on some fake eyelashes that were so heavy and long they made her eyes look half-closed, and she kept touching them like she was making sure they wouldn't fall off. Hardy mumbled something and the girl – Amanda, he thought her name was – giggled nervously, looking out over the river. Finn crept nearer, wanting to hear what they were saying, and concealed himself behind an old hollowed-out tree. When he looked again, they were kissing.

He had never seen his brother kiss anyone, not like that, the way their heads were bobbing in tandem. He had often wondered what it would be like to kiss someone properly, had even tried it on the back of his hand once, though he'd found the experiment unremarkable. Watching Hardy now, he recognised within himself a jealousy, both that his brother got to kiss someone real, but also that he'd chosen to be there with her instead of him.

He watched, scarcely blinking for not wanting to miss anything, as Hardy's hand rubbed up and down her thigh, watched as it crept beneath her clothing and travelled up her stomach, the fabric bunching against his wrist the higher it went, so that her skin was revealed. And then his hand was at her boob, and Hardy moaning in a way Finn had never heard before that made him embarrassed.

Amanda suddenly pushed him away and got up, straightening her clothes as she glanced at Hex Cottage. 'Someone in that house could see us.'

Hardy rolled onto his back, looking wistfully at the sky.

'What's this?' Amanda nudged the food waste bag with her foot.

'Nothing,' he said.

She picked the bag up. 'Why do you have so many sandwiches?'

Hardy propped himself on his elbows. 'My dad made me take them.'

Finn had forgotten about his own sandwich, and he saw now that the bread was flattened where he'd clenched it too tightly, its contents having oozed onto his fingers. He put it down on a root and wiped his hand on his trousers, his skin sticky.

Amanda bit into one and pulled her face. 'Oh my God, there's so much jam!' She laughed – Finn knew she was laughing at Daddo, felt the hot snap of it at his ears – and then she threw the rest of it into the river.

Hardy stood, and for a second Finn believed that he was going to get angry with her, that he was going to tell her she shouldn't chuck things that didn't belong to her, things that Daddo had taken the time to make with his own two hands, especially not into the river, which was many things both good and unnerving, but wasn't there for her to treat that way.

But Hardy took the bag from her, saying, 'We can use them as bait.' And then he began tearing off large hunks of sandwich and tossing them into the water, where they floated worthlessly in the milky green shallows.

'When we catch the fish,' Amanda said, 'we get to take them home, right?'

'You're not technically supposed to,' Hardy said, coolly. 'But my dad does it all the time.'

He had offered it up so easily.

'Really?'

'Goes at night so no one sees him.'

She snorted. 'Your dad seriously sounds so lame.' She said this almost gleefully, and then kissed his cheek.

'I know, right,' Hardy smirked.

'I've got an idea.' She poked him in the stomach. 'We could make sushi with whatever we get. Like we had on our first date.'

'Nah, I'm going to eat whatever we catch like I'm Gollum,' Hardy said. 'I'm biting into it straight from the river.'

'*Gross*,' she said. 'What about its guts and stuff?'

'I'm not even going to kill it first,' he continued.

Amanda picked up the rods, smiling at him. 'You're such a psycho.'

It shocked Finn, how much the person he was watching was not his brother, but someone alien to him, and he knew this person, whoever they were, would surely be unrecognisable to Daddo as well. He was gripped by the urge to get far away from there and began to run, back through the woods and along the road, until finally he reached the allotment and burst through the gate. Daddo was at his plot having a cup of tea with the others, and Finn darted clumsily among the grid of vegetable patches, hadn't stopped running before everything began to pour breathlessly from him.

Daddo put down his mug and stood in one movement. 'What's happened?' he said, alarmed. 'Is Hardy all right?'

But Hardy was not worthy of Daddo's concern. 'No,' Finn shouted, 'he's a prick.'

Bemusement or perhaps impatience settled into Daddo's face, and he did not take his eyes from Finn as he said, 'Emir, mate, can I use your shed for a minute?'

Emir, who was sat in one of the plastic chairs, said, 'Help yourself.'

Daddo took Finn into a small shed that smelled of soil and rubber gardening gloves. He sat Finn on an upturned bucket, and stood with his arms crossed, so tall his head grazed the roof. 'Out with it.'

He told Daddo all of it, every single part of what had happened.

When he was finished, Daddo blew heavily from his mouth. 'Okay.' He nodded slowly, contemplating everything he'd just been told. For some moments, he looked beyond Finn, staring into the back of the shed. 'Okay,' he said again, finally. 'Come on, then.'

Finn followed behind Daddo, snaking between plots to the weathered gate and then up the road, but instead of continuing on to the woods, they stopped at Daddo's car, which was old and rusty blue.

'Where are we going?' Finn said.

'To think.'

As they drove from the village, Daddo had the radio on too loud, and after a while, Finn said, 'Are you mad at Hardy?'

Daddo didn't answer, didn't even look at him. Regret began to churn in Finn: that maybe he shouldn't have told Daddo *everything*, that maybe he'd landed Hardy in it because of Amanda, or that he'd hurt Daddo by telling him about the sandwiches and the river and the things they'd said about him.

When Daddo pulled over, it was into the car park of a pub called The Merry Wherrymen. Daddo got out of the car without saying a word, and as Finn followed, he saw that they were on the river again. Inside, Daddo ordered a pint of Adnams lager from a woman at the bar. The two of them made polite, disinterested chat about the upcoming pub quiz as the woman pulled the tap, and Finn realised that it had been a long time since he'd seen Daddo talk with a woman, and speculated then whether he could have a secret girlfriend like Hardy did. But Daddo was always at home, or working at the retirement place, or else he was at the allotment, or with them, fishing, and he couldn't imagine where somebody might fit into the little space that was left. It hadn't occurred to him before that Daddo might be lonely.

They sat outside on a patio that jutted out over the water. The pub was on a steep bank, and Finn was able to see across the complete width of the river in a way he hadn't before. From here, he could see great swathes of bright green weeds trailing down the river like streamers, could see all the logs and stones beneath the surface.

And then Daddo began talking. 'A river is made up of different currents.' He pointed over the railing. 'See the way the water's moving just there? That's your seam. It's where the slower water in the eddies meets the faster current running through the middle, and then further out, closer to the bank is your shallows. Smaller fish spend all their time in the eddies, but some fish, the bigger fish, the ones we want, hang out along the seams with their bodies in the gentler current and their heads in the main channel so they can catch anything whizzing by.' And then he said, 'It's the most rewarding part of a river, where the different parts meet like that, where the fish are in two flows. Now you don't need me or anyone to show you where the fish are.'

'That's not true,' Finn said. 'I'm still too short.'

Daddo had a swig of beer, then pushed it across the table to him.

Finn grinned at it.

'A mouthful,' Daddo said.

He lifted it to his lips, the glass slick with condensation.

'And not a big one either.'

It was bitter and tasted like socks.

'People are a lot like rivers,' Daddo said.

Finn rolled his eyes.

'What do you think of the beer?'

'I like it,' he lied.

'I'll get you a lemonade,' Daddo said.

Hardy was in the living room when they arrived home. He must have been just sitting there, waiting for them, because the remote was still tucked behind the TV. He looked at Finn and then at Daddo, wanting him to speak first, so that he could gauge whether he was in trouble or not.

'You're back,' Daddo said. 'How was the river?'

'Good,' Hardy said. 'Fine.' He looked again at Finn, intently this time. 'Are you feeling better?' He spoke slowly, knowingly. 'Because you didn't eat your sandwich. You left it on that tree root.'

The jam was still smeared on Finn's trousers.

'Anything happen?' Daddo said.

'What do you mean?' Hardy said. 'Like what?'

'Oh.' Daddo shrugged. 'I suppose I don't know.'

Finn watched the pair of them. It was as if the shape that had existed between them before had changed and they were feeling their way round its new, unfamiliar contours.

'Finn left early,' Hardy said.

'That's what he told me.'

Finn stared at the floor.

When Daddo spoke again, it was quietly, deliberately, so that every word became in a way magnified. 'He told me a right story, in fact.'

'Did he?'

'Said he was on the riverbank and about fifteen feet or so from him, was it, he saw something that really upset him.'

He heard Hardy inhale deeply, as if bracing himself.

'He said,' Daddo continued, 'that a great big log bobbed to the surface—'

Finn saw the confusion on Hardy's face before he'd even registered for himself what Daddo just said.

'And it was all slimy and smooth and mottled green, isn't that right, Finn?' He glanced at Finn, and then turned again to Hardy. 'And then he sees right there on the end of this log, the end that's closest to him, an eye. And it was bulbous and staring, he said, but it was intelligent too, like it was weighing him up, watching him as if he was something to see. And he knew by the size of its fat cheek and its long, pointed jaw, that it must be enormous, monstrous. It could only have been the same beast of Norfolk that I once had the misfortune of laying eyes on: the Hesket Hag.'

Hardy must have been relieved that he wasn't in trouble, because he started to grin.

Daddo's voice changed then, and Finn knew that Hardy wouldn't go unpunished after all. 'You think she's funny, do you? Terrible things have happened to people who've underestimated the Hag. She's a horrible devil of a fish, a wolf in pike's clothing, and she's—' He moved away from Finn, closer to Hardy. 'She's bigger than anything in this part of the world should be, bigger than any man; some say bigger than a shark. She can go wherever the water takes her, and one river connects to another, of course – the Wensum, the Yare, all the way up the Bure – the Broads are her hunting ground. She waits among the weeds and silt, stalks the unsuspecting holiday boats, just waiting for someone to fall in. No one's ever managed to bring her reign of terror to an end because whenever someone goes out to try, she's never found, like she can disappear at will, but she's always there, watching, biding her time. And she's older than anyone alive by centuries—'

'That's impossible,' Hardy said, his voice nervy in the way it always was these days, but undercut with something more; unease maybe. 'Fish don't live that long.'

'Sure,' Daddo said. '*Normal* fish. But the Hag is something else, something from another age. The Hag, well, she was actually a woman, once upon a time, who the men of Old Hesket decided to kill for being a witch. They chucked her in the river to drown her, but when they pulled the ropes out again she wasn't tied up in them any longer, and her body was never found. Legend has it that her fury at being unjustly murdered was so powerful it transformed her into a monster, doomed to haunt the river for the rest of time, with nothing to do but exact her revenge. And that's why she likes to get men most of all; young lads like yourselves, too. I'm surprised you've not heard the old tales about her?'

Hardy shook his head.

'*Have a paddle and watch out for a shadow*, they used to say,' Daddo continued. 'The scariest part, in my opinion, is that she has rows of bladed teeth and a muscular, crushing throat, with strange, scale-less skin that blends into the water, just like Finn said, all dark green and brown, practically invisible; you wouldn't know she was there until it was too late. The perfect predator, really.

'*Take a dip and she'll have a nip.*

'Twenty years ago, in fact, a woman told the paper that the Hag took her wolfhound on a summer's evening, sucked it under as the poor dog went in after a stick and turned the river red. They say the Hag once dismembered a swimmer, a whole leg down her thick throat, bitten clean off, that she eats children whole so there's nothing left of them to bury. But her favourite meal, according to all the old boys at the pub, is to rip open the stomach so that a person's guts trail out as they try to swim away to safety, so she can eat them alive from the inside out.

'*See the water stir and you'll be taken by her.*

'We're just lucky that Finn wasn't using his rod, or she'd have pulled him in by his line. All she could do in this instance was sink below the surface, down beneath the weeds, to disappear and wait for her next opportunity to feast.'

Finn's heart was thumping so loudly it seemed impossible

that no one else should hear it, each wallop surging cold fear through his body. After a little while, Hardy said quietly, 'Is that actually what he told you?'

Daddo crossed his fingers behind his back so that Hardy couldn't see them. 'Captain.'

Hardy looked approvingly at Finn. 'Good story.'

Emir

Emir had already been at the allotment for hours, arriving in the earliest morning before the birds had even begun to stir, because the crocuses blossomed at dawn and wilted as the day progressed, and the bright red stigmas required plucking with tweezers, one by one, just as the flowers were beginning to open. It was precise work, collecting saffron. If he harvested too early, the stigmas wouldn't be developed enough; too late, and they'd be shrivelled. It had been his grandmother, Nazanin, who taught him it was best to pick before the sun came up. He'd been sent to spend the summer with her when he was twelve, during his parents' divorce, and found the little courtyard outside her home filled with old yoghurt pots and plastic tubs, chipped teapots, a mop bucket, and in them all, the spindly leaves of saffron crocuses just waiting to emerge.

He didn't understand Iranian and she didn't speak English, the two of them relying on a rudimentary kind of sign language they developed, but gradually, the affection that passed between them transcended language, and came so easily and surely it was as if it'd been buried within their shared DNA, waiting only for a season of their prolonged company to emerge, luminously and in full bloom. What he remembered most of those weeks now was warmth in all of its incarnations, and the distinctive aroma of saffron as Nazanin cooked rice on the little stove by the window that overlooked the courtyard. She'd been affection personified, her faraway home a haven from his parents' bickering. But the time came too soon for him to return to England ahead of the new school year. His grandmother wept at the airport (and it *was* weeping, more mournful than crying), as she kissed his head over and over, not wanting to let him go, and the smell of her hair, like cooking spices, like saffron. He'd tried his best to console her, convey his promise to return with a series of ineffectual gestures. He couldn't have known that he'd not see her again after that, but he recognised traces of her now in the stigmas – the solace of their aroma, the vibrant beauty in their colour – and in this small way she felt alive to him again.

Sunrise over the allotment had been a layer cake of turquoise beneath an electric orange, the softest pink, and then, edging the horizon, the most intense yellow sun, before the sky became one large cauliflowery cloud, all blush and mauve and lovely, and by the time Paul and Mr Thatcher arrived, the sky was bright, and Emir had an egg cup of fiery saffron, ready to be taken home and dried. Norfolk, he'd discovered, was a surprisingly hospitable place to grow saffron, on account of its relatively dry summers and cold winters. This year, in particular, had been exceptionally hot and without rain, and the allotment saw a glut of produce: tomatoes ripening on the vine and more courgettes and runner beans than anyone knew what to do with; greenhouse crops abounded, like cucumbers and sweetcorn and peppers and aubergine; Jules even managed to grow melons.

Emir was relieved when the cooler temperatures finally arrived so that the crocuses could begin to produce their leaves (though it was odd to feel the autumn chill and still be in a drought), and now, in late October, they were blooming on schedule. But he knew that surely, after so long without it, rain was not far off. He'd seen the clouds, hulking and low, pause threateningly over Hesket as if contemplating whether this was the spot to unburden themselves, but so far, apart from a single afternoon of mist-like rain two weeks ago, they'd thankfully always thought better of it and moved on. His crocus bulbs were susceptible to rot if the ground was too wet, and a substantial enough shower might damage the delicate flowers before the saffron was fully developed. He hoped the weather would continue to cooperate a little longer, so that he could harvest every morning until all the crocuses had finished with their flowering, and then he would welcome the rain, as heavy and as long as it liked to come. He carefully placed his harvest on the small potting table in his shed, and went to check on Myrtle.

Myrtle was Hurley's tortoise. She was kept at the allotment and allowed to wander round occasionally when she wanted to stretch her legs, so some people had built tiny Myrtle-proof fences round their plots to keep her from eating their lettuce. She'd been hibernating in an old cardboard box since shortly after Hurley's death, and Emir had been putting leaves of rocket in there just in case she woke up, because it was her favourite kind of green to pillage; there were now sad, wilted piles of it around her shell. He wondered sometimes whether Myrtle would miss Hurley when eventually she stirred again, and if tortoises were capable of grief.

He joined the others at Paul's plot. Paul made them tea using the camp stove he kept in his shed and passed around a packet of chocolate digestives. He was wearing his favourite t-shirt again, which had a cat wearing a captain's hat on the front. It was Emir's understanding that Paul had made himself the unofficial head of the allotment some years back, when he set out a circle of white plastic chairs like Arthur's Round Table, making his plot the place to gather for a cup of tea; he'd even fashioned a barbecue out of an old washing-machine drum. Paul asked how the saffron was coming along and Emir shared his worry about the rain, and then they all complained about British weather always doing the opposite of what was wanted of it, while they covered themselves with biscuit crumbs. Mr Thatcher pinched some tobacco from a tin and stuffed his pipe. He insisted that people call him *Mr Thatcher* instead of his first name, Richard (though Paul sometimes called him Dickie behind his back), and always addressed people by their surnames. He wore a tweed gilet without exception, even in summer, and slacks tucked into his Barbour wellies, and was the only person he'd ever seen who actually used a smoking pipe.

'Did you see yesterday's *Norfolk Times*?' Paul said.

Emir blew on his tea, shaking his head.

Paul disappeared into his shed, emerging moments later with the paper folded open and handed it to Emir, who read aloud:

Cursed Village Fears Development Disruption

Today, Hesket is a single-road yawn-and-you-miss-it Norfolk village, small enough it would be a hamlet were it not for the medieval church. But centuries ago, it was a different place entirely, one troubled by witchcraft and death, and a curse that, according to one local woman, still lingers to this day.

It is unknown when exactly the local woodland was given the name Spry Wood; presumably it was a goodwill gesture to honour the Hesket women who were killed during the witch trials, although why it was only the final victim, Alice Spry, that was given this distinction, remains a mystery. Very little is known about the unfortunate souls accused of witchcraft in the area. Most details about Hesket's trials have been lost to history, and it was only by visiting county record offices that we learned the names and fates of all nine women:

Prudence Bishop – hanged by the neck until dead;
Lydia Chapman – hanged by the neck until dead;
Susan Chapman – hanged by the neck until dead;
Mary Harris – hanged by the neck until dead;
Hannah Tippet – hanged by the neck until dead;

Margaret Crabb – hanged by the neck until dead;
Mary Witton – hanged by the neck until dead;
Ruth Hooper – hanged by the neck until dead;
Alice Spry – drowned, body never recovered.

In an unusual turn of events, current-day residents are citing Hesket's dark past as a major reason not to continue with an ongoing development project, fearing that the new housing is to be sited on 'cursed' ground . . .

'Cursed ground?' Mr Thatcher said dubiously. 'What rubbish.'

'My thoughts exactly,' said Paul.

'Whoever's written this—' Emir glanced to the top of the article for a name. 'This Rio person hasn't included anything about the environmental impact,' he said, scanning the two remaining paragraphs. 'Nothing about how they're felling a perfectly healthy woodland for money.' He dropped the paper at his feet. 'There's not even any more interesting historical information. It's all just folklore.'

Mr Thatcher scoffed.

'I wonder if they've found bones. Caldwell might have covered it up to avoid being shut down again,' Emir said. 'Those woods could technically be a mass grave, if all these women were buried there.'

'Tell you something.' Paul leaned in, his voice lowered conspiratorially. 'My boy Finn said he saw Jack Moody at the site, cutting down trees.'

'No!' Mr Thatcher exclaimed.

Mr Thatcher lived in one of the neighbouring hamlets and had never shown much interest in the development until this very moment.

'Do you think Walter knows?' Emir said. 'At the village meeting he seemed pretty adamant that Jack was against it.'

'Poor Mr Moody,' Paul said. 'I'd be fuming if it was one of my boys.'

'Too right,' said Mr Thatcher.

'Walter asked me the other day if I'd seen a chainsaw around here, said Jacky-boy's had gone missing from the garden shed. Won't be able to do much felling without one of them, will he now?'

Mr Thatcher nodded. 'I suppose the silver lining is that Hurley didn't live to see such treason.'

Emir looked over at Hurley's patch, at the neat rows of autumn vegetables still in the ground. 'What's going to happen to his plot?'

'The council'll give it to the next person on the list,' Paul said.

The allotment was the only one between Hesket and the village of Swanton Morley – which was where Emir worked as a primary school teacher – and there was always a waiting list.

'They'll inherit a good crop then,' Emir said.

'Actually,' Paul leaned back in his chair, 'council comes and digs it over so it's a blank canvas for the next tenant.'

'But that's wasteful.'

'What about his things?' Mr Thatcher said. 'His tools?'

'His personal effects?' Emir added.

'Council takes what they want, destroys the rest.'

'Can they do that?' Emir said. 'Can they just *take* things?'

'I've seen it happen before.'

'But that's outrageous.' Mr Thatcher took an indignant drag on his pipe and puffed, his words coming out in a cloud of smoke. 'If that's not robbery, then I don't know what is.'

Paul shrugged. 'Robbery or not, my friend,' and then he held up a biscuit to show them all, 'it's how the cookie crumbles,' and put the whole thing in his mouth.

'What should we do?' Emir said. 'Hide his things from the council?'

'And do what with them?' Mr Thatcher said.

'Use 'em,' Paul said.

'But then aren't *we* just taking his things?' Emir said.

'It's either us or the council.'

'Jones here has a point.' Mr Thatcher used the stem of his pipe to emphasise each word. 'A damn good point. Why should the council, who didn't even know the man, steal his tools? Hurley would want them to go to the people he knew.'

'That's right.' Paul got to his feet, dusting bits of biscuit off his lap. 'He's got a brand-new petrol tiller in that shed over there, state of the art. Very expensive. Something he knew I couldn't afford on my salary, but he was telling me just before he died that I should get one, so I think he'd probably want me to, ah, make use of it.' He nodded at Mr Thatcher. 'And I know you've had your eye on that tumbling compost barrel.'

Mr Thatcher coyly placed the pipe between his teeth.

'I can't deny it.' It was as close to giddy as Emir had ever seen him.

'I think we're all forgetting his family,' Emir said. 'What if they want his things?'

'They've no idea what he's got,' Paul said dismissively.

'So you *think*,' Emir said. 'But we have no way of knowing that.'

'Listen, he wasn't particularly close with them.' By this point, Paul had picked up his garden hoe and was leaning on it as if it were a staff, perhaps to make himself appear more authoritative. 'I highly doubt they even knew he had a plot.'

'He told me once that he grew peas for his daughter; she'd have known.'

'Sure.' Paul said this as if it was information he'd already had. 'But the *rest* of them.'

'Well,' Mr Thatcher said slowly, 'I've personally never seen anyone here with him. Have you?'

Emir had to admit that no, he hadn't.

'And we know he lived alone.'

'And his daughter lives in Lincolnshire,' Emir countered. 'It's not far.'

'I thought she was in Liverpool,' Paul said.

'I'm sure Hurley told me once his brother is out west,' Mr Thatcher continued.

'What about the ex-wife?' Paul said.

'She's Polish, I think.'

'What's that got to do with anything?'

'Brexit. They've got to leave, don't they?'

It was, Emir assumed, a tasteless joke, but then Paul looked at him uneasily.

Mr Thatcher saw Paul glancing at Emir, and said, 'What's the problem? I'm stating a fact.' And then he too looked at Emir.

It occurred to him that each of these men expected something from him, a reaction, even though Emir himself was originally from Sheffield, and his parents were not Polish.

Paul, still gripping his hoe, gestured at Emir as if to say, *I'll handle this one, mate.* 'Look, she obviously doesn't live here in Hesket or we'd have seen her, so moving on then.'

'Well, in that case,' Mr Thatcher said, 'it seems to me that it's unlikely the family will be aware of exactly what Hurley owned with regards to his plot. And it therefore seems to me also, that they won't know if there's anything missing when they come to clear it out.'

'If they come,' Paul said.

'*If* they come,' Mr Thatcher agreed. 'And we know that the council will arrive regardless to pillage poor Hurley's belongings. So I think we *all* know, really, what the best course of action to take is.'

Paul said, 'I was actually just about to make that point myself, but thought I'd let you continue, ah' – he made a rolling motion with his hand – 'onward and that.'

'What about Myrtle?' Emir said.

'I doubt she'll care,' Mr Thatcher quipped.

'Pop her in the meadow?' Paul suggested. 'I'd take her for my boys, but it'll end up being muggins here who'd have to look after her.'

'But she might wander over to the development site,' Emir said. 'What if she gets crushed by a falling tree?'

'The council will probably give her to the RSPCA,' Mr Thatcher said. 'Sorted.'

The thought of Myrtle living out her days in a miserable cage without any grass beneath her feet or rocket to munch sounded to Emir like an exceptional kind of cruelty. 'I'll take her,' he said. 'I'll take Myrtle.' He could show her to the kids in his classroom, even build a lesson around her now they were finishing with their foray into local history.

'That's it settled then.' Mr Thatcher slapped his knees jovially. 'We'll reallocate Hurley's stuff. I'll take the compost barrel, Jones will have the tiller, and the tortoise has a home with you.'

'Hold on,' Emir said. 'I mean, those tools are probably worth hundreds of pounds.'

'I agree,' Paul said. 'We don't do this unless it's equal.'

'Fine by me,' Mr Thatcher said. 'You'll just have to take something more valuable then, Salami.'

'Sal*man*i,' Paul said, which Emir appreciated, because it was awkward and, he felt, could sometimes come across as a bit impolite to correct someone himself.

Mr Thatcher held up his palms, as if excusing himself. 'What do you need?'

'I don't know.' Emir looked at his plot. 'I just need it not to rain on my saffron, I guess.'

Paul snapped his fingers. 'You should have the greenhouse.'

'Excellent idea, Jones,' Mr Thatcher said.

That Emir should come into possession of a greenhouse

filled him with a sudden enthusiasm, like a time-lapse of a tight bud blossoming eagerly into an open flower. At 8x10, it would not cover all of his crocuses, it was not so large as that, but it would save a good amount from ruin if it chucked it down, and that was enough. 'All right,' he said. 'It can go directly on my plot.'

'Brilliant.' Paul struck his hoe against the ground as if it were a judge's gavel. 'Now it's *properly* settled. A tiller for me, compost barrel for Mr Thatcher, and Emir has the greenhouse and custody of Myrtle.'

'What about everything else?' Mr Thatcher said.

'We should share it with the others,' Emir suggested.

'Correct,' Paul said, as if Emir were on a game show. 'We'll divvy it up; we're not greedy.'

Paul and Mr Thatcher began to talk excitedly as they rose from their chairs.

'Wait,' Emir said. 'If we're going to take Hurley's things, then I think we at least have to pay our respects to him.'

'Honour his memory.' Mr Thatcher nodded. 'Good idea. Classy.'

They all agreed it was the right thing to do. Paul sent out a text to the allotment WhatsApp, so that the other plot holders could not accuse them of leaving anyone out:

> Dear cultivating comrades, an informal service will be held in memory of our sadly departed friend, Hurley, today at 11 a.m. (regrets for short notice). Tea and biscuits provided.

Simon, of Simon and Geoff, responded first, asking if Paul could clarify what he meant by 'service', because that implied the vicar would be there, which would not be very informal. Paul answered that Rev. Eileen Wright would *not* be there, and that all he'd meant was they were just going to say a few words in Hurley's memory. Simon replied that, anyway, they couldn't make it. Walter also said he couldn't go because he was accompanying Nell Riley on a day out at Blickling Hall, as did Jules, who was away in Somerset, and Helen, who explained she'd have appreciated more warning because neither she nor her fourth husband, whose name no one could remember, were able to come now that they'd already made plans for the day. Mr Thatcher wrote that he'd most definitely attend, though his RSVP was for show more than anything, since he was of course already there. The others didn't respond at all, which Paul told Emir privately he found inconsiderate.

The three of them sat at Paul's plot and made small talk about rainbow chard and the horrors of tomato blight until the appropriate time was finally upon them.

'Well then.' Mr Thatcher checked his watch. 'I don't think anyone else is bothering. How shall we do this?'

Paul scratched his beard. 'I suppose we just take it in turns to say something nice about him.'

'Is that it?' Emir said. 'I thought it would be more of an event.'

'What else is there?' Paul said. 'It's not like we can have a proper funeral without Hurley's ... you know ... remains.'

'We could bury something in his place,' Mr Thatcher suggested.

'That's an idea,' Emir said. 'It might be a bit less ... sparse.'

Emir looked at Paul, who was bouncing his leg in a restless way. 'You lot've read my mind because I was just thinking that myself,' he said. 'I was just about to say it.'

They decided on Brussels sprouts, because Hurley loved to eat them and was the only person on the allotment other than Walter to actually grow any. They cut the largest stalk and chose a suitable place next to his greenhouse, because that was where Hurley had spent most of his time.

After months of drought, the ground was dry and hard, and very difficult to pass a spade through. Even Paul, who was the largest of them, and was himself shaped like a spade, had to stamp repeatedly on the blade to get anywhere. Paul insisted he should dig the hole himself, which meant Emir had to watch him until he'd had made it symmetrical enough, while Mr Thatcher held Hurley's stand-in, with its dozens of tight green globes winding up the stalk, and large floppy leaves that shuffled in the wind and hid most of his face and torso.

Quiet fell between them, and Emir's thoughts turned to what Hurley would make of them holding a funeral for his Brussels sprouts, which led him to wonder if Hurley could somehow see them now.

When Paul finally announced that the grave was ready, Mr Thatcher carefully laid the stalk within it, tucking its leaves around like a sort of burial shroud, so that nothing poked out. Paul removed his flat cap and held it solemnly against his belly. 'A damn good grower, Hurley. His heirloom tomatoes never split, not a single one in all the years he grew 'em. He was the king of tomatoes.'

'Hear, hear,' Mr Thatcher said.

Paul threw in a clump of soil. 'I only wish I'd asked him what the secret is.'

Emir thought it was probably just enough sun, water and fertiliser, like everything else. Paul clapped him on the back and said, 'Your turn, mate.'

'Hurley ...' Emir hesitated. He tried to think of something suitable to say but found himself unable to recall in that moment any interactions with Hurley at all, couldn't think of a thing other than the fact that he was standing there dumbly, saying nothing, as though all his thoughts had evaporated completely, and so he only said, 'He'll be much missed by us all. And he was very good to Myrtle.' Then he threw in his dirt, and it sprayed across the sprouts.

Mr Thatcher stepped forward, clearing his throat. He then delivered a ten-minute speech about the various interactions he'd had with Hurley at the allotment, some of which didn't sound like they'd actually involved Hurley at all, particularly the anecdote about aubergines. When at last he scattered his clump of soil and crossed himself, Paul and Emir filled in the grave.

It was decided that because the council could turn up at any time, it was best if they got Hurley's things all sorted then and there.

It was an odd sensation, being in someone else's shed, which was so unlike his own and so particular to Hurley. It felt clandestine and electrifying that he was there to strip it of everything. Here he was, standing in the shed of a dead man, rooting through his things – things that until recently Hurley himself had touched – and it felt as if the items still held part of Hurley and were in a way alive with him. He wondered, as he piled a hose and various small tools into a crate, if this were actually what Hurley would want, to be divided up and scattered among them like this. When Nazanin died, Emir was the main beneficiary in her will. By then, he was in his teens and had been shocked to learn that what little she'd had went to him. More than anything, there'd been an overwhelming guilt. It was him that she'd bestowed her life to in death, and what had he given her, other than a broken promise to return?

In his periphery, he suddenly became aware that he was no longer standing alone, but was instead in the presence of a shadow in the back corner of the shed that made him freeze, made a shudder swim up his spine. It was human-shaped. Dark and gaunt and startling. And even though it was faceless, he could feel it staring at him, was sure that any second it would reach out a horrible, withered arm and seize him—

But then Paul appeared at the door and the spell was broken, and Emir turned and found that the spectre was nothing more than a raincoat hanging by its hood.

'Bit spooky in here, eh?' said Paul, looking around.

Mr Thatcher peered over Paul's shoulder. 'What's the hold-up?'

'Nothing.' Emir lifted the crate of things he'd collected. 'Just getting organised.'

Mr Thatcher made an impatient noise. 'Well, let's get on with it.'

They emptied Hurley's plot, darting back and forth like ants, one after the other, their arms laden with netting and tools and watering cans.

Geoff, of Simon and Geoff, showed up about five minutes in. 'Simon only just mentioned about Hurley's thing...' He trailed off at the sight of Mr Thatcher, coming out of Hurley's shed with a stack of seed trays, and the large pile they had accumulated by the door. The three of them looked nervously at one another as Paul explained about the council.

Geoff took the wheelbarrow and incinerator.

'Walter could probably do with some of the pea canes,' Paul said. 'And the cold frame, bless him.'

They left the horticultural fleece folded thickly beneath a pair of expensive Japanese secateurs at Jules's plot and carried the raised beds over to Helen's. Paul also took the trowels for his boys to use. He said the others didn't deserve anything because they'd ignored his WhatsApp.

They pulled all the leeks, cabbages and Brussels sprouts until there was nothing left in the ground, and Paul distributed these evenly among them, like a king giving hand-outs to peasants.

'No sprouts for me, thanks,' Emir said. 'But I'll take one of the leaves for Myrtle.'

'Poor Myrtle,' Geoff said. 'She's no idea.'

Myrtle hadn't stirred from her hibernation despite the commotion around her. Emir carefully moved her cardboard box from Hurley's shed to his, and set her next to his egg cup of saffron; there was hardly enough room on the potting table. He draped the large leaf across her shell like a blanket, then closed the box again. He would earn his new greenhouse by taking care of her, would go to a pet shop in Dereham tomorrow and buy some straw to help keep her warm, and when she awoke, whenever that might be, he'd see if she might like a thread of saffron to eat. He regretted that he'd not been able to think of anything to say about Hurley earlier, that he'd not given him a decent goodbye. They'd had numerous conversations, some quite long, but even now he could not recall what a single one had been about. Brussels sprouts, maybe.

Geoff knocked on the doorjamb. 'I'm off now,' he said, and then continued to stand there. 'That's a nice old greenhouse you're getting.' He folded his arms. 'Hurley made it himself, actually, the year he got his plot. Cut the metal and glass to his own specifications and everything, so it's one-of-a-kind.'

'Really?' Emir began to feel badly then. He'd never properly looked at it before, assuming Hurley had simply bought it from a garden centre.

'Course, it's a bit tatty now.' Geoff leaned in and said quietly, 'If you ever want to part with it, let *me* know first, okay?' He glanced outside at the others. 'You should probably get back out there. Things are getting a bit heated.'

Emir looked through the shed's grime-streaked window. It was obvious Paul and Mr Thatcher were having an animated discussion; Paul was gesturing at the greenhouse and then pointing over to Emir's plot. Mr Thatcher was shaking his head, smoke billowing as he drew continuously on his pipe. In his hurry to get outside, Emir nearly knocked his cup of saffron to the floor, and his heart lurched at the thought of his harvest mixing with soil and dust and whatever else, ruining it all, and he moved it as far from the edge of the table as Myrtle's box would allow.

A large pane of glass had been removed from the greenhouse and was now propped against Emir's shed along with a small pile of nuts and bolts.

'It just seems silly,' Paul was saying, 'to do all that only to move the thing a few yards.'

'You *cannot* just pick up a greenhouse and move it,' Mr Thatcher said, the pipe clenched between his teeth. 'It simply cannot happen.'

'Maybe not any great distance—'

'No distance. There is no distance in which it can be done.'

'What's going on?' Emir said. The wind was beginning to pick up, blustering across the meadow and over the squat hedge of the allotment.

Mr Thatcher looked as though he wanted to smack someone. 'I AM. TRYING. TO EXPLAIN TO JONES. THAT ONE CANNOT JUST' – he mimed picking something up on the left of him and then putting it down on his right – 'A GREENHOUSE.'

'Well, obviously we won't just' – Paul mimicked what Mr Thatcher had just done. 'Obviously we won't do that. But it doesn't make sense to spend all day taking it completely apart and then rebuilding it when it's only just going right there. No sense at all.'

'Okay.' Emir adopted the same diplomatic tone he used on the Year 6s when they were squabbling. 'Let's just all calm down and think for a minute. I'm sure there's an efficient way to do this that we can all agree on.'

'Listen,' Mr Thatcher said, 'I know exactly how to deconstruct and reconstruct this. It'll take no time at all if I direct every—'

'Here we go,' Paul shouted. 'I *knew* it. You've wanted to run the show all day.'

'Oh, for God's sake,' bellowed Mr Thatcher.

'You can't stand that I'm head of the allotment.' Paul jabbed a finger at him. 'You've been itching to usurp me and now you think you've got your chance, eh, Dickie? Shame on you for exploiting the death of poor old Hurley for political gain.'

'How dare you!' It was Mr Thatcher's turn to jab now. 'You *aren't* the head of the bloody allotment! There *is* no bloody head of the bloody allotment!'

'Here's what we're going to do.' Emir had to raise his voice just to be heard. 'We are ...' He did not actually have a plan. 'Going to ... we're going to deconstruct the top half of the greenhouse, and then move the bottom half as one piece. There.' He crossed his arms, hoping it might make him appear like he knew something about what he was suggesting. 'Compromise.'

'Excuse me?'

There was a woman standing behind them all, materialised as if from nowhere.

What struck him first was just how pale she was; he'd

never seen anyone so pale as her. She wore a long, old-fashioned dress and had dark hair that he at first mistook for a mourning veil, the way it hung about her shoulders and flew across her face in the wind, and for the briefest moment, he considered the possibility that she was a ghost. He might not have been the only one, either, because Mr Thatcher's pipe fell right out of his mouth.

'I'm looking for Leonard Hurley's space,' she said. 'I'm his daughter.'

Emir was fairly certain that he heard Mr Thatcher whisper, 'Well, shit,' as he retrieved his pipe.

For too long, none of them said anything else. Remorse enveloped Emir with a swiftness he'd not experienced since teenhood. What were the chances that after two weeks of nothing, someone would come looking for Hurley's belongings the same day, the same hour, they were taking them?

'He might have gone by Len?' she offered. 'The council said it's plot C, but none of them are labelled.'

Paul cleared his throat loudly. 'Yeah, that's, um, that's this one right here.'

She looked at the newly emptied soil, at the three neat piles of sprouts and leeks, and at Hurley's empty shed, with it door still wide open. And then she looked at all of them, gathered at Hurley's greenhouse with its missing glass panel, and at the conspicuous mound of dirt near Emir's feet, which was of course where they'd buried the effigy of Hurley.

It was clear that she wanted some clarification on what

she was seeing, but Emir couldn't bring himself to speak, too stunned by guilt and their rotten luck.

'And whose is this plot?' She pointed towards the pane of glass, so obviously missing from Hurley's greenhouse, leaning against Emir's shed.

Out of the corner of his eye, he caught Mr Thatcher pointing slyly towards him with his pipe, and he knew that he'd been exposed.

'And who are you?' she asked Emir.

He stepped forward, extending his hand as he mumbled his name.

She hesitated, before reaching her arm towards him from where she stood rooted, leaning in so that she could grasp his fingers briefly, before straightening again.

'I'm sorry about your dad,' he said. 'I'm really very sorry.'

She nodded. 'Did you know him well?'

'Sure,' Paul said. 'I mean, sort of; well enough.'

This must have been the wrong thing to say, because she scowled and looked around again. 'What's going on here?'

'We had a memorial for him,' Emir said. And then, because he thought she'd appreciate it, he added, 'We would've invited you, but we didn't know how to get in touch.'

'I've been at his house for the last week,' she said curtly. 'So you can't have tried very hard, can you?' And then she put her hand to her mouth and looked to the ground, and made a noise, like a hiccup or a sob. Mr Thatcher moved as if to soothe her, but she held up her palm to stop him. When she spoke again her voice was weary. 'So you didn't know him very well but you had a memorial.' She was shaking her head.

'Sounds about the same as me, then.' She said this bitterly, more to herself than to them. 'I don't know.' She looked at Emir with disbelief, could not seem to stop shaking her head. 'I don't know what I'm doing this for.'

Emir saw clearly that there was anger in her face, but more than that, he recognised the acute and tremendous pain that trails loss like a phantom. 'He mentioned you; he talked about you a lot actually.' That last bit was in fact a lie; Hurley had not been much of a talker at all now that Emir really thought about it, which was probably why he'd not been able to recall anything Hurley said. The conversations they'd had tended to be one-sided, and Hurley had usually expressed his opinion in the form of grunts or, most often, laughter (even at insensitive moments, like someone's asparagus being decimated by slugs, which wasn't a very nice thing for him to do, actually), that Emir remembered as a distinctive and peculiar kind of laugh, because it sounded a lot like a yowling cat. The woman was staring at him, perhaps deciding whether or not to believe what he'd said, so he continued, 'Said he grew peas because you liked them.'

'Oh.' Her face softened a fraction. 'We grew them together when I was really little. I never saw much of him after that; he wasn't much interested when I was a teenager.' She inhaled sharply and held it, and when she let it go again it came out jagged. 'This whole situation is just so ...' She pressed her fingers to the bridge of her nose and closed her eyes, as if willing herself not to cry. 'I mean, I didn't even know he liked tortoises, but there's a massive stack of tortoise books at his house that now *I* have to deal with, that I have to pack into a million boxes and then break my back loading into the car all by myself so I can donate them somewhere. *And* there's figurines. *Figurines*, for God's sake!'

Emir could, at least, clear this up. 'Myrtle.'

'Hmm?' She sniffed distractedly.

'The tortoise,' Mr Thatcher said.

'What?'

'Myrtle,' Paul said. 'The tortoise.'

'What tortoise?'

'Hurley's,' Emir explained. 'He has a tortoise called Myrtle.'

A strange look came over her then, and she stared at him, wide-eyed, and slowly said, 'Myrtle is *my* name.'

'Well,' Mr Thatcher said. 'That's ... interesting, isn't it?'

'I don't understand.' Myrtle put her hands to her head, bunching her hair in her fingers. 'What does that mean? Why would he do that?'

'I don't know,' Emir said, lamely.

'Oh my God,' she continued, more to herself than to them. 'He called it *Myrtle*?'

Emir looked at Paul, who shrugged, and then back at her. 'Do you want to see?' he said.

They all crowded into Emir's shed, which was not an easy thing to do considering its size, and he opened the large box on his potting table.

Myrtle-2 peered in at Myrtle-1, blinked hard a few times at the motionless tortoise before her, and let out a wail. 'Oh no,' she sobbed. 'Is it dead too?'

'She's hibernating,' he said. 'She's asleep.'

'Oh,' Myrtle-2 whispered, sounding relieved. She wiped her face on her sleeve. 'Why's she got a leaf on her?'

Paul and Mr Thatcher peered quizzically into the box.

'We'll leave you two alone,' Emir said, and ushered the others out.

They gathered again at Paul's plot.

'It *is* weird,' Paul said quietly. 'Naming his tortoise after her like that, when he didn't have much to do with her.' He put the kettle on. 'Apart from the peas, of course.'

'That's what I was just thinking,' Mr Thatcher said. 'I was just about to say that.'

'I don't think it's weird.' Emir slid lower in his chair, so that his neck was resting against it. 'Things are named after people all the time.'

Geoff came hurrying across the allotment then, motioning erratically to get their attention. 'Simon's only just told me,' he shouted. 'The wally! Apparently the daughter's here clearing out Hurley's house. Says he knows cause she asked him when bin day is.'

They tried frantically, all three of them, to make him stop shouting, but he must have mistaken their furious waving to mean that they couldn't hear him, because he only continued, louder now. 'Do you think she'll come here? Will she want his incinerator?'

When he reached them, they explained in furtive voices about Myrtle-2 and how she was now in the shed with Myrtle-1.

Geoff looked mortified, and whispered, 'Do you think she heard me?'

Paul, who was aiming a teabag at a mug like he was in a beanbag toss, hissed, 'I don't see how she couldn't.'

When Myrtle-2 emerged, she was carrying the cardboard box. It was clear she'd been crying again because her eyes looked puffy and heavy-lidded, like the eyes in Renaissance paintings.

'I'm going to go now,' she announced. 'I'm taking Myrtle.'

It made sense, of course. It was right that she should have something too, but all the same, the tortoise's departure felt too unexpected and sudden; perhaps selfishly, Emir hadn't thought about the possibility that he might lose Myrtle-1 or the companionable life together he'd begun to envision since deciding to adopt her.

Myrtle-2 stared at them all, before casting a last brief eye over at Hurley's pillaged plot, and then left as abruptly as she'd come.

'Well, that's a relief,' Mr Thatcher said, after she'd closed the gate behind her. 'I thought she was going to kick off.'

'As soon as we've had this cuppa, we should get the greenhouse moved and be done with it before anyone else can come sniffing around,' Paul said.

There came a startlingly loud and violent noise from Hurley's plot then, that made them all turn and look just in time to see the greenhouse collapsing in on itself, the glass shattering as panes collided and exploded into fine pieces, and the rusted metal frame bending horribly and sounding for all the world as it did so like Hurley's yowling laugh echoing loudly around them and reverberating in cackles across the meadow.

*

The knocker on Hurley's front door was shaped like a brass trowel, and Emir struck it three times, dislodging a few flakes of peeling green paint as he did so. He'd found out the house number from Geoff shortly after the Myrtles left the allotment, and then walked over, standing now on the step next to an autumnal tangle of shrivelled rosehips and yellowed leaves. He didn't wait long before the door swung open, and Myrtle-2 was looking back at him, visibly puzzled.

'I forgot to tell you that Myrtle loves to eat rocket,' he said. 'The tortoise, I mean.'

She only squinted at him, and said, a little apologetically, 'You've told me your name ...'

'Emir Salmani,' he said. 'I brought this for you.' He held out the little cup from his shed. 'It needs drying before you can use it.'

She peered at its contents. 'What is it?'

'Saffron,' he said. 'Picked this morning.'

'I see.' She took it from him carefully, as if she recognised it as something precious. 'I didn't know you could grow it here.'

'It's very settled in this climate, actually.' He cleared his throat self-consciously. There were boxes piled in the room behind her, swaths of newspaper on the floor. 'In fact, it's been cultivated in England for hundreds of years.'

'Is that so?'

'The conditions just need to be right.'

'Like growing it in a greenhouse, for example?' She raised her eyebrows at him.

His ears grew hot, and he cleared his throat again. 'That fell down, actually.'

She looked sternly at the cup in her hands – he wondered, wildly, if she might throw it at him – before quite unexpectedly, there appeared a lopsided and sympathetic smile on her face. 'Then I suppose I should say that I'm sorry for your loss, Mr Salmani.'

The next morning was much like the one before it. Emir was again at the allotment early, and in the cool, watery light he inspected his saffron crocuses. Nestled among rows of chive-like leaves, a few blossoms were nearly mature enough for another round of harvesting. He would come again to collect more saffron before work in a couple of days. He sat and listened to the birds singing, the light broadening incrementally as the hour ticked along, and then Paul showed up, whistling.

'Going to try out my new tiller before the others come,' he said, rubbing his hands together excitedly. 'Don't want the ones who didn't get anything asking questions.'

'How can you, though?' Emir said. 'You've still got veg in the ground.'

Paul looked suddenly impish, gesturing to the plot they had stripped bare only the day before. 'I'm going to run it over Hurley's. I just want to have a play with it.'

'Well, let me know when you've had your fun and I'll pop the kettle on.' Emir watched him wheel the machine to the barren plot and pull the cord, the motor rumbling to life, throaty like a lawnmower. The blades began churning lumps of earth and spitting it out in fine crumbs. Paul leaned back to counterbalance the welly of it as he pushed the machine forward, and then, almost immediately, came a spluttering, like the tiller had sliced over something it shouldn't have, something dense and wet, and Paul cut the engine quickly, inspecting the blades, the surrounding soil.

'Hey, Emir,' he said loudly.

'Are you in need of a tea break already?' Emir said. 'You've only been at it a minute.'

'Can you come here, mate?' His voice sounded odd, no longer excited but confused – alarmed, even.

Emir, curious, did as he was asked, and Paul pointed to the ground before them, tracking his finger in a sweeping arc across it. 'See?'

'What?' Emir saw nothing at first, only bare soil, and just as he was about to ask Paul what exactly he was meant to be looking at, a lurching movement caught his attention, and then another and another.

What should have been an empty expanse of earth was not empty at all, and what Emir had assumed were large clods on its surface were in fact toads, dozens of them, and as he stood there, confused, he felt something at his foot, and looked down at another toad, a huge one, heaving itself over his shoe on its way from Hurley's plot, and then he realised there were more of them staggering unwaveringly across the allotment, disappearing under the hedge, and as he stood on his tiptoes to see over the top of it, he saw a line of toads marching across the meadow, along the track of grass flattened by the tree surgeons' machinery, reaching all the way towards the woods.

'Where are they going?' Paul was still staring bewilderedly

at Hurley's plot. 'Why are there so many of the bleedin' things?'

'Maybe they were hibernating?' Emir said, trying to make sense of what he was seeing. 'But...'

Paul looked at him. 'But what?'

'It's still cold. Myrtle will sleep until the end of winter. Shouldn't the toads do the same?'

The toads seemed in a frenzy, scooping soil as hurriedly as they could and flinging it wantonly behind them, determined to heave themselves out of the underground hollows they'd been lying in, like zombies rising from so many tiny graves.

'Is it, er, normal for them all to pick the same spot to hibernate?' Paul said.

No, surely not. Emir looked back at the woods, its trees appearing from this distance to be huddled together, so that they had a conspiring look to them, and he watched the toads walking clumsily towards it, their limbs landing in heavy, jerking movements like marionettes, as if controlled by something beyond themselves.

And then Paul suddenly recoiled. 'Oh,' he said, covering the lower part of his face with his jumper. 'Do you smell that? It's awful.'

Emir turned again towards Hurley's plot and was met with a wall of foul stink that wafted up from the ground after the toads, treacle-thick and putrid, like rotting meat.

Rev. Eileen

The light was already beginning to change by the time Eileen arrived at the station to catch her train home. She could not be late getting back today; her son was coming round for a last-minute farewell dinner, and she'd promised Morris that she'd be there before Christopher arrived.

Eileen was seated on one of the benches outside because the air smelled cold and clear, and she enjoyed how it made her cheeks feel like cool marble when she removed her glove and touched her warm fingers to them. At one end of the platform was a family, a hum of excitement around them. On the nearby bench, two teenage boys were holding hands, their knees slouched towards one another. One of the boys had a choppy green mullet. It was he who caught her gaze and shifted, whispering something so that the other glanced at her. Eileen smiled, but by then they'd already turned away, and she did the same, not wanting them to think she was gawking or – aware of the clerical collar she wore – that she was in some way disapproving.

She supposed that she should let Morris know that she was on her way back to Hesket now, but thought again of the conversation they'd had that morning as she was leaving the house – the way he'd said to her, *This is important, Eileen* – and decided not to.

She'd returned to those words all day: sometimes she recalled them as having been reproachful, and at others they took on a more pitying tone, but no matter how they came, they would not settle and be done with. Morris liked to joke that being a vicar wasn't a bad gig as far as hard work went, that it was really only on Sundays that Eileen had anything to do. He would say this to their friends in order to elicit a chuckle, to her parishioners at community events, and at any other time her occupation came up. *I'm only kidding*, he'd placate her later. *I know it isn't true.* But still, he would say it. It did not matter that Eileen was never home before seven most days, that she oversaw four parishes, which meant four times the number of services to give and parish accounts to keep, community projects and fundraising campaigns to oversee, of parishioners to visit, traversing the long and winding country lanes on her bicycle (she felt guilty using the car for only herself, when there were far too many of them on the road as it was). The meetings were daily. She sat on the board of governors for two schools. There was the scandal of the development to deal with (she'd seen the plans for the houses, modern and large and concrete, completely incongruous with their surroundings), and now an article had come out that made the people of Hesket sound like superstitious bumpkins, and she would have to meet with the journalist next week and implore her to write a new piece, spoon-feed her how damaging an impact the development was having on the local ecology. Lately there'd been a rancid stench hanging around the village, and people were complaining that a septic tank or sewer must be leaking, and of course it was she who was expected to keep on at the council to investigate. And on top of it all was the constant pressure of dwindling congregations, and the peril of beautiful old churches becoming fallow so that no one cared any more when they began to crumble, and this, more than anything else, compelled her to continue. Faith was important. History was important. But people and communities were the most important. And Eileen knew that in some way she was important, because she kept as much of it going as she could; people needed her, and who was she to deny them? Just now, for example, she'd come from visiting a man who was having complicated surgery tomorrow; he'd moved last year and was under the guidance of a different vicar now, a man, but even still, it was she who he asked for in his time of worry. She was entitled to six Sundays off a year and four weeks' paid holiday, and she held a sense of personal satisfaction – or, if she was being frank, it was pride – that she'd never once used them all, had never even taken the full week of rest she was allowed after the intense demands of Easter and Christmas. But her efforts did not go unnoticed or underappreciated. She never went long without a note of thanks, and every year there were little parcels of homemade Christmas cake and carefully wrapped chocolates. She was trusted with their most vulnerable moments, but equally, with some of their happiest, and what a gift both of those things were.

Eileen checked the station clock; the train wouldn't be long now, and she sighed quietly to herself. It was of course understandable, perfectly understandable, that she should be upset; neither Morris nor Christopher could surely fault her that. It seemed inevitable that tonight she would be the interloper in her own home, her own family, and all because of a woman whose name she didn't even know. *I don't care what she's called*, she'd said, when Morris tried to tell her. *If he wants me to know her name, then he can tell me himself.*

Morris had called her ridiculous.

Just then, a young woman walked onto the platform and came to a stop in front of the boys. She was carrying a bouquet of flowers wrapped with a big yellow bow, and wearing a jumper that had a cat on it with oversized eyes and its chin on its paws, smiling, or grimacing, Eileen could not tell which.

The young woman had a long drag of her cigarette before moving nearer to the boys, saying something to them, and she had an expression of boredom as she looked along the train track, into the distance. The boys glanced at one another uncertainly, before one of them bent to tie her shoelace. She flicked her spent cigarette onto the platform, and then fished one of those awful vapes from her bum-bag and began to suck on it. When her laces were tied, she picked up the cigarette butt without another word, letting out a large, sweet-smelling cloud as she deposited it into the bin, and took a few more steps along the platform to pause by Eileen.

She glanced at Eileen's clerical collar, and then produced a piece of paper from her bag.

'Can you tell me where this is?' She had a soft voice, but it was authoritative all the same. She held up a sheet from one of those cheap invitation pads used for children's parties. It was bordered with colourful balloons and confetti, and had been filled out in neat handwriting.

> *You are invited to the party of: Sally S.*
> *At: 29 Conway Road, Sheringham*
> *On: Friday, 7th November*
> *Arrive by: 5 p.m.*
> *Until: 9 p.m.*

Eileen had not been to Sheringham in years, and even then, she'd never deviated from the promenade of shops that led directly from the train station to the beach. She handed back the invitation. 'I'm sorry. Let me just ...' She began to root through her backpack, searching for her phone so that she could map it.

'Can you take this for a sec?' The young woman held out the bouquet, which Eileen, with her hands still filled with the things she'd removed from her bag, took. The young woman had another drag of her vape, expelling it through her nose as she began to leisurely root through her bum-bag. When she'd found what she was looking for – she pulled out a pack of fruity gum – a sparkly green pen cap fell to the platform, and she watched it bounce before gently kicking it away.

'All right, Zoey?' A man from the nearby family had taken a few steps towards them. He had a large belly and wore a beaten-looking leather jacket. 'Where are you off to, then?'

The young woman – Zoey – said, 'I'm going to a party.'

'I love a good party, me.' And then he bounced his elbows and shoulders awkwardly in a sort of silly dance. He stopped when he noticed Eileen looking, his eyes catching her clerical collar, and he said to Zoey, 'How's your dad, then?'

'Fine.'

'He still sore I beat him at darts the other night?'

Zoey shrugged. She popped a piece of gum in her mouth, then returned the pack to her bum-bag.

'We've got tickets to the Pavilion,' he said. 'You been before?'

'Once,' Zoey said. 'It was okay. They got my nan on stage and made her squawk like a chicken.'

'Ha!' He clapped his hands, rubbed them together.

'They ask for volunteers.'

'Cheers for the tip.' He winked. 'Tell you what, I'll make one of them lot do it and take a picture for you.' He thumbed over his shoulder to his family, and then glanced again at Eileen before saying, 'So where's this party, then?'

Zoey walked over to him, handing him the invitation, and the two of them joined the others.

Eileen realised too late that she still held the bouquet, and examined it for the first time. There were white lilies in it, the kind used in funerals. The powdery orange stamens were still attached, blemishing a couple of the pristine petals yellow where the pollen had fallen. Eileen hooked her fingers round each one, pulling so that they all dropped into her cupped palm before she deposited them beneath the bench. She smoothed the ribbon, adjusted the card that was tucked between flowers to make the handwritten *To Sally* more visible, and then set them on the bench so that Zoey could retrieve them later.

There'd been a boy in Christopher's class years ago who had Down's syndrome. They'd gone to each other's birthday parties, and she'd found him sweet and shy, though she couldn't remember having talked with him, now she really considered it. And thinking on it, as she returned her things to her backpack, she didn't know what had become of this boy, or when, if, he and Christopher had stopped being friends. She decided that she would ask him at dinner this evening, if only to suspend the no doubt ceaseless conversation about Christopher's plans.

Tomorrow morning, Christopher was moving all the way down to Penzance to be with a woman who Eileen would only be meeting for the first time tonight. He hadn't even told her he was seeing this woman; it had been Morris. *Apparently they met online*, Morris said. *She's a doctor and he's in love.* Eileen had expected Christopher to tell her himself, but after waiting weeks it became clear that he assumed the information had been relayed to her second-hand, and that that was good enough. At least Morris had agreed that the whole thing was too abrupt. They'd never even heard of this woman, and now she was taking him about as far away from Norfolk as a person could get before they left England all together.

A train pulled into the station, not hers, but one bound for the coast. The doors opened but no one got off. She watched the boys beside her stand and head towards the nearest carriage, didn't realise she was staring so intently until the boy with the haircut waved in a pointed way that made her blush. When she looked up again, the platform had completely emptied. The flowers were still on the bench. 'Oh dear,' she said aloud. She gathered her things and approached the train, hoping that Zoey would realise she'd forgotten the bouquet and appear at the door. She scrutinised the windows, waiting, unsure of which carriage she'd be in. The train made an urgent beeping noise – the doors were going to close. Eileen hesitated, glanced at the flowers in her hand, the envelope with its shaky handwriting, and then stepped onto the train. The doors hissed closed. She lingered in the precipice between carriages, unsure of the choice she'd just made, as the train pulled itself to motion. Beyond the window, the station slid lazily by, until quite abruptly it was replaced by a bank of vivid green; it was shocking, just how green the rest of Norfolk was in comparison to Hesket.

The second carriage was much fuller than the first, and she held the flowers overhead so that they didn't swipe the headrests as she passed, walking slower than she wanted to, self-conscious in her examination of every filled seat. All Eileen could think to do was nod and smile awkwardly if they caught her looking, as she tried not to knock into anyone each time the train lurched. She found Zoey in the next carriage, still with the family from the platform.

'Excuse me.' Eileen presented the bouquet to the table. 'You forgot your flowers.'

The table quietened. Zoey looked first at Eileen and then at the flowers, recognition settling into her face.

A woman at the table took the bouquet from Eileen and held it to her nose. 'Well, these are lovely, Zoey.'

The man peered briefly up from his phone. 'Hurry up and take them from her, Zoey. Don't want Carol getting any ideas.'

Carol tutted and passed them to her.

Zoey snapped her gum. 'Thanks.' She inspected the flowers briefly, then put them down on the table and looked out of the window.

Eileen did not know what she'd expected – some enthusiasm at the bouquet having been returned, or that her efforts might be acknowledged more gratefully. But then, Zoey was not to know that because of her she would now be late. 'Well,' she said. 'Have a wonderful time at your party.'

Zoey was still gazing intently out of the window. The sun was below the western horizon now, its residual light steadily dimming the fields.

'Zoey,' Carol said. 'Hun, the vicar is speaking to you.'

Zoey turned to look at Carol, who gestured towards Eileen with her head.

'Thanks,' Zoey said again.

Eileen swayed in the aisle as the train hurtled onward.

'It'll be good fun, won't it?' Carol pressed. 'The party.'

'Yeah,' Zoey said, nodding. 'They've got, like, *Fortnite* and *Call of Duty*, so it should be pretty good.'

The girl next to Zoey moaned. 'No waaaay, Mum won't let us play those.'

'No, I won't,' she said. 'Far too violent, Vicar.'

'They're not that bad,' Zoey said. 'It's mostly just guns.'

'See?' The girl slunk in her seat. 'I told you, it's *fine*.'

'Zoey,' Carol said.

'Just don't drink too much, Zoey,' the man quipped. 'We know what you're like with the booze.' And then he laughed, pleased with himself.

The slouching girl joined in, looking at Zoey, who very clearly tried to suppress a smile as she turned to the window again.

'Kev,' Carol scolded. 'A little more decorum in front of the vicar, please. And you...' She motioned to her daughter. 'Say hello to the vicar.' When her daughter didn't respond, she said, 'Now please, Hannah.'

'But no one else is,' she protested.

Carol turned to her youngest girl. 'You too, Grace, come on.'

'I *did* already,' Grace said.

Carol shook her head, and said to Eileen, 'So contrary, the pair of them.'

The train pulled in at the next station, and people began shuffling towards the doors.

'This is us already.' Carol stood suddenly, ushering the children to follow. 'Everyone up, quick-quick.'

Eileen had assumed they were going to Sheringham, that they would walk Zoey to where she needed to go.

Zoey turned to watch them leave. 'Bye.'

'Take care, hun.' Carol waved at Zoey, and slung her handbag over her shoulder. 'God bless, Vicar.'

'I don't think she knows where she's going, though,' Eileen said.

Kev zipped up his coat. 'You been to your friend's house before, Zoey?'

Zoey snapped her gum again. 'Yep.'

'Vicar.' He nodded once at Eileen, and then was gone.

'*Do* you know where you're going?'

'Sally's house.'

'Because you were asking how to get there earlier.'

A flicker of impatience crossed Zoey's face.

Eileen knew she should get off. But even though the departure warning sounded, she didn't move. And then the doors closed, and the train continued, and she sat herself at the table across from Zoey. She upended her backpack on the seat next to her, retrieved her phone in the jumble. 'May I see your invitation?' Eileen said. 'So that I can look up directions for you.'

'I think it's fine,' Zoey said flatly. 'Really.'

'It wouldn't hurt to double-check your route.'

Zoey ignored her.

'It's not – it's not that I think you don't know,' Eileen lied. 'It's just something I always do when anyone asks for directions.'

Sighing, Zoey sat back against her seat. 'I suppose.' She sounded dubious but slid the invitation across the table.

Eileen copied the address into her phone. 'It's only a seventeen-minute walk from the station. Have you got a pen?'

Zoey began inspecting her fingernails, nipping at the skin around them. 'Nope.'

Eileen rummaged through the pile beside her but found nothing. 'Well, it's an easy enough route.' She showed Zoey her phone. 'See? Just up Station Road—'

Zoey pulled out her vape.

'I don't think you can use that here.'

Zoey made an annoyed sound and dropped it back into her bag.

'Have a look at this, though.' Eileen angled the phone closer to Zoey. 'If you remember it, then you won't get lost.'

The phone vibrated once in her hand, and Zoey's eyes darted to the phone screen and lingered there a moment, before she returned to her nails again. 'I won't get lost.'

'Do you have maps on your phone?'

'No, I don't,' Zoey said firmly. 'I don't need it.'

Eileen could feel the train already beginning to slow again.

'You got a text, by the way,' Zoey said.

Eileen checked her phone. It was from Morris:

nearly home?

If she started back now, she'd only be half an hour late.

The train pulled into another station, and Zoey peered outside again to watch the people queueing to get on. A man, eccentrically dressed in a bowler hat and waistcoat, sat down at the table across the aisle and began to read a book titled *The Happy Medium: Trials and Tribulations of My Psychic Life*. Eileen put the phone down on the table, covering the screen with her hand, and she and Zoey sat quietly. The lily stamen had left Eileen's fingers a nicotine yellow, like her father's had been after decades of smoking cigarettes. It was her strongest memory of him.

Morris was a very different kind of father than her own, much more emotional, certainly much more attentive, perhaps overly so. He'd coddled Christopher as a child, accommodated his every impulse, had given in easily to tantrums and excused poor behaviour in his teenaged years. Even now, he went out of his way to do things that Christopher himself was capable of doing. And he'd indulged Christopher's ridiculous relationship with that woman. Eileen was not a panderer, but she believed that she'd been a good mother. She, more than Morris, had been the one to do bath time, to put Christopher to bed, to pick him up from school. She'd never missed a recital or a game, had made sure he visited the dentist and read books. It was she who carefully chose and wrapped every Christmas and birthday present, who'd helped him find his first flat. Yet it was Morris who he'd told, Morris who – in Eileen's mind – their son so clearly favoured, and it angered her; she'd not been above admitting as much to Mo either, who'd only said he felt sorry for her, if that's what she believed.

The carriage filled with more passengers, the chatter louder now, and the train moved onward. She would wait until she was on her way back to call and explain her tardiness.

'It'll be dark in hardly any time,' Eileen said. 'How about I walk with you when we get to Sheringham? I've got directions, and you wouldn't want to rely on a stranger if you get lost.'

'You're a stranger,' Zoey said.

'I'm Eileen,' she corrected.

Zoey raised her eyebrows.

'I'm a vicar.' Eileen touched her collar.

'I *know*,' she snorted. 'I'm not blind.' It was difficult to tell her tone, whether it was playful or irritated.

The seat upholstery was bristly and rough, and prickled Eileen through her cotton trousers, irritating her skin. She gestured to Zoey's jumper. 'I've got two cats, you know. Three, if you count the one that hangs around the graveyard at St Giles's church.'

'I prefer dogs.' She smoothed her jumper. 'And this is actually a kitten.'

'Ah.'

A woman wearing a tracksuit walked past them, talking loudly on her phone.

Zoey leaned forward, her arms on the table. 'Is the church haunted?'

'Pardon?'

'There's graves.'

'Well, I don't know,' Eileen said. 'I don't believe in ghosts.'

Zoey chewed her gum. 'There's one in the Bible.'

Eileen smiled. 'It's not a literal ghost. Not like what you're talking about.'

'So you don't have any, like, scary stories?'

'No.'

She looked disappointed.

'Actually,' Eileen said, remembering, 'my son said he saw something once. He used to come to the church with me when he was a child to practise his violin. He was very gifted. I'd be shut away in the vestry mostly – meetings and paperwork – and he'd be out in the nave, and I'd hear him playing in the background. And it was lovely, really, the two of us getting to spend time together, before children get older and lose interest in their paren—'

The phone vibrated against the table once, twice. Zoey glanced at it, then settled her attention back on Eileen.

'Well anyway, one day he's practising his scales and then suddenly there's this almighty scream, I mean it really was—' Eileen made a wide gesture with her hands. 'Within seconds he came running in, pale as anything. He was crying. Sobbing, actually. And he collided into me. I remember his head hitting my chest, and his knuckles were absolutely white around his violin. It took a while for him to be able to talk properly so that I could understand what had gone on.'

She paused. It was not a story she'd shared before. She had thought about it now and then, could still see that look on his face as clearly as the day that it occurred. Zoey was no longer chewing her gum, the whole of her attention fixed solely on Eileen; the man across the aisle had stopped reading his book and was now openly listening to her story. The phone vibrated again, continuously this time – someone was calling. Without looking to see who, Eileen slipped it from the table and into her backpack.

'He said it happened when he was playing, looking out on the pews as usual, performing for a pretend audience. One moment they were empty and the next he saw a hooded woman sitting in one of the rows, watching him.'

'Oh shit,' Zoey whispered. 'Just watching?'

Eileen nodded. 'Apparently it was grinning, the woman, and ...' She paused dramatically, ran her finger along the inside of a lily petal, down near the centre where it was green and irregularly textured, like the dull pins on a music box.

'And what?'

'He said there was rope around her neck.' She motioned to her lower jaw. 'And there were maggots or something falling out of her rotting skin.'

For a moment, Zoey appeared anxious, disturbed, but then her fear dissipated, and she grinned. 'That's so creepy.'

She imagined Zoey walking into her party later, telling them all the ghost story she'd just heard from the friendly vicar who'd made sure she got there okay. It was the kind of thing they might talk about all night, that might even become part of their mythology. *Remember that vicar who told me about the haunted church?* It wasn't haunted, of course; just a figment of a child's imagination, and more likely, another ploy for attention. Morris had made Christopher a difficult child, demanding of their time, as if it was owed to him, which to a degree it was, of course; they were his parents. But then Christopher had refused to return to the nave, insisting that he remain in the vestry with her, which at the time had been impossible. She had meetings scheduled; it would have been inappropriate and unprofessional for him to stay in the room. Whenever she pictured him from that day, it was outrage she saw on his face rather than fear, and this in turn had made her dig her heels in even more.

'I couldn't help but overhear,' the man across the aisle said.

'But my, what a tale. Your poor boy. If my job . . .' He paused, corrected himself. 'If my *calling* as an international clairvoyant has taught me anything, it's that sometimes when spirits present themselves unexpectedly, it can be quite traumatising for those who witness them. I could speak with your son—'

'No,' Eileen said. 'No, thank you.'

The man glanced at Zoey, raising his eyebrows, before returning to his book.

'I'd never go there again,' Zoey said.

'Christopher did, the following day.'

'You *made* him?'

'Well.' Eileen tapped her fingers impatiently on the table. 'I had to work, and like I said, you know, he couldn't just stay at home.' She was surprised at how defensive she felt.

'How old is he?'

'Now? Thirty-one.'

'That's old.'

'It's not old,' Eileen said.

'I'm twenty.'

'Well, I'm nearly sixty-four, and that's not old either.'

Zoey looked unconvinced, and then offered her a piece of gum.

'Thank you,' Eileen said. She took it, even though she did not particularly want it. Zoey watched Eileen put it into her mouth and then took another piece for herself, adding it to one she already had. As far as Eileen could tell, the gum had no discernible flavour other than overly sweet.

The train began to decelerate again, and the two of them looked out the window into the dusk. They were at

Sheringham now. It was less a station and more a single platform, with only three benches beneath as many lit streetlamps. Behind these were bushes, and the dark roofs of houses, and in the distance, a Tesco.

'Have you got any cigarettes?' Zoey asked as they stepped onto the platform. She had the bouquet sandwiched between her arm and torso, flowers at a precariously downward angle.

'I don't smoke,' Eileen said. And then, because she couldn't help herself, 'It's bad for you.'

Zoey rolled her eyes. She pulled out her vape, dragging on it deeply, and then exhaled a large sickly smelling mist that drifted momentarily along the platform before evaporating into nothing. The temperature was considerably chillier here on the coast, and Eileen buttoned up her coat.

'Are you cold at all?' she said. 'I might have a scarf with me.'

Zoey shook her head as she had another drag. Eileen checked her phone. On the home screen were two messages and a missed call from Morris:

> Christopher's come early. Says they need to leave sooner because he has some bits to finish packing, fyi

and,

> where are you?

It was just after 6 p.m. She should have been well on her way home by now.

'This way, let's not dawdle.' Eileen marched along the platform, weaving through the collection of people waiting to board the train. She stopped by the car park and waited, Zoey following at a languorous pace, more concerned with her vape than keeping up. 'Do you want me to hold those for you?'

She did not resist when Eileen gently pulled the bouquet from her.

'We're late.' Eileen continued walking, peering at the map on her phone every few yards and pausing so that Zoey would catch up. Overhead, shadowy gulls were calling, and beneath that, a constant faint sound in the distance, like wind or traffic. The further they walked from the station, the more Eileen could hear it – the North Sea. She checked the map; they were not that far from the beach, and if she were to take the next road left, the sea would be there in front of her, restlessly rolling in and retreating again.

Eileen eventually eased her pace to match Zoey's, and they walked together in silence until the shops gave way to houses, the streets quiet. She had long since stopped chewing the gum.

'You should help that ghost,' Zoey said.

'How do you mean?'

'Tell it to enter the light,' Zoey said. 'Like they do on those paranormal shows.'

Eileen rarely had the chance to sit in front of the television and wouldn't have watched programmes like that anyway.

'It's there for a reason,' Zoey continued. 'And maybe it's stuck.'

'Oh?' Eileen tried to hide her amusement. 'What sort of reason?'

'Unfinished business. Revenge, guilt; that kind of stuff.'

'I didn't know ghosts could feel guilt.'

'Well, they can.'

They fell into silence again.

When they finally got to the turning onto Conway Road, Zoey paused. She began waving at a boy who was approaching from the opposite direction. 'Hey,' she called. 'Hi, Harrison.'

He was dribbling a football and glanced up at the sound of his name. He had a lean face, with pimples dotting his chin and forehead, and looked sixteen, seventeen. 'Hey, Zoey.'

Zoey had another drag of her vape as he crossed the road and joined them.

'Were you just at practice?' she said.

'Yeah.' He picked up the ball, tossing it gently between his palms.

'Ready for the Battle Royale tonight?' Zoey said excitedly.

'You know it.' His voice pitched on the second word. 'Maybe don't bring a sniper rifle to a shotgun fight this time, though.'

The two of them laughed, the joke obscure to Eileen, and she shifted impatiently, the bouquet's cellophane wrap crinkling audibly now they were away from the crowd.

Harrison looked at her. 'Hi?'

'This is Sally's little brother,' Zoey said, before gesturing over her shoulder at Eileen. 'That's Eileen.'

'Sooooo ...' She saw him register the collar at her neck. 'How do you know each other?'

'The train,' Zoey said.

'Zoey asked for directions,' Eileen clarified.

He scoffed. 'You know where we live,' he said to Zoey. 'You've been over, like, a million times.'

'Not on the train, I haven't,' Zoey said.

'It's fine.' Eileen smiled reassuringly. 'I don't mind. Happy to help.'

'Well, it's just literally there.' He pointed down Conway Road. 'So she's all right from here, aren't you, Zoey?'

'Yeah,' Zoey said. 'Thanks.' And then, without even a proper goodbye, she turned the corner onto Conway and was gone, just like that.

Her exiting seemed too abrupt, too impassive. But Eileen still held the bouquet, which meant that she could follow Zoey and rectify this act of deflation, could tell her, at least, to take care.

'Her flowers.' Eileen began to go after her, but Harrison held out his arm.

'It's all right,' he said. 'Give 'em here.' He took the flowers from her, and looking at them, and at Eileen, he said, 'You really didn't need to come all this way. She could've carried these herself.'

'I wanted to make sure she'd be all right.'

'Yeah,' he said, 'but it's kind of . . .' He trailed off, as if considering whether or not to say whatever it was that he was thinking. 'You know?'

'No actually,' Eileen said. 'I don't know what you mean.'

He raised his eyebrows. 'Sometimes she lets people do things for her, that's all.' He gestured to the bouquet, as if to demonstrate his point. 'Like I said, she could've obviously carried these.'

He had momentarily stunned the words out of her. If it was a joke, it was a crude one. And if he meant it, which she suspected he did, well, that was even more tactless and malign a thing for him to have said. 'I think a bit more sensitivity is needed, young man.' She was aware of how old she must appear to him in that moment; she sounded like her father, who had always used *young lady* when he scolded her.

His expression changed then, so that he looked exasperated. 'She's got her own flat, you know. She has a job and a driver's licence, and she's going to uni.' He smirked openly at her. 'Think about *that*.' And then he too left her standing stupidly there, with her erroneous presumptions, on the corner in the dark. She took the gum from her mouth, and held it, horribly pink and glistening in her palm, until she could find a bin.

It was Christopher she called on her walk back to the station. As the phone rang out, she thought again of that day with him in the church, and wondered for the first time if she had done the right thing; it was not defensiveness she'd felt earlier on the train, but the stirrings of guilt, like silt rising from a riverbed. From somewhere, church bells began to ring. There was a sudden pressure on the crown of her head then, almost like fingernails on her scalp, that raked the skin and moved her hair, and she spun quickly round, thinking it was Zoey trying to scare her in return for the story she'd told on the train, or that she'd come to say goodbye after all, but there was no one there; the road was empty all around, the streetlights washing it in a mellow glow, and not a single gull. She continued walking, quicker now, the phone pressed again to her ear, but after a few fretful moments it rang out to voicemail, and she hung up and tried Morris. He answered after the fifth ring, sounding like he'd just been laughing.

'Where on earth are you?' he said.

'I'm on my way home now.' She didn't know how often the trains ran from Sheringham. 'I won't be long, an hour and a half, I should think.' There was chatter in the background, a woman's sharp laughter. 'I'll definitely be there within two.'

Morris relayed the message. She could hear Christopher's voice but couldn't tell what he was saying.

'Can't you get here sooner? They're heading off in fifty or so minutes. I texted you.'

'Is he angry?' Eileen said. 'Let me speak to him.'

'He's fine,' Morris said.

'He must be furious,' Eileen continued. 'And I completely understand if that's the case.'

'He's not. Really. We're having a good time.'

'Surely he is, though.'

'Eileen, I'm telling you, he doesn't care.' There was another shrill giggle. 'Susanna is *lovely*.' He said this deliberately, she knew, because she'd not asked about her. 'It's a shame you aren't here to meet her.' She was probably sitting in Eileen's seat at the table, silently judging her absence, waiting to commiserate with Christopher later.

'We were just talking about the lack of rain we've had here. There's lots in Cornwall, apparently; I told them to send us some when they get there.'

A desperation overcame her then. 'Is he really leaving that soon?'

Morris must have covered the receiver with his hand, because his voice sounded muffled when he said, 'Eileen wishes she was here.'

She heard Susanna respond with a sound like, 'Aww.'

'Mo,' Eileen said.

The sound of Christopher then, saying something she couldn't make out, and then all of them laughing.

'Mo,' Eileen said, louder. 'He isn't staying?'

'He can't. But he's invited us down to Penzance for Christmas, which isn't too long off if you miss him tonight.'

'Christmas?'

'I know,' Morris said. 'But hey, maybe you could take it off this year. Wouldn't that be nice?' But even as he said it, his conviction faltered, and Eileen knew he understood that she could not, that her work would not allow it, and that in offering, Christopher had understood it as well.

Arthur

On the day Arthur received the invitation, Eileen had come round as usual on her fortnightly visit, and he insisted like always that she sit in the only armchair, that he was fine on the floor.

'I tried baking a focaccia,' he said, when she'd asked how his week had gone. 'Disaster. I'll stick to sourdough.'

'You know, I tried getting Christopher into that sort of thing,' she said. Christopher was only a handful of years younger than Arthur, who was thirty-six. 'My mother was Irish and used to bake a loaf of soda bread before we went to school.' They were sat near the window overlooking the Wensum, and she was watching the water, a wistfulness on her face.

'I'll make you some,' he said.

She seemed not to hear him. 'I think she probably did it because the smell was enough to get us out of bed without any hassle, but now it just means that homemade bread makes me think of her and growing up in that house.'

He'd been about to repeat his offer, when she said, 'There's a woman who might call you, a journalist, to get your opinion on the development. I hope you don't mind but I told her about your proximity to the site. It's very important that you don't talk about a curse or whatever nonsense she might bring up with you, only emphasise the historical and ecological importance of the woods. I told her that myself, but it wouldn't hurt to double down. We need to be taken seriously.'

He raised his eyebrows. 'There's a curse?'

'Of course there isn't,' she scoffed. 'It's a silly bit of folklore that someone from the village – and I thought she had more sense – has decided is now factual history. It's been nothing but an irritant, to be honest with you.' She sounded fed up, which was unlike her, and as if conscious of this herself, she said in a more cheerful tone, 'Anyway, what else have you been up to?'

'Oh,' he sighed. 'Same old, really. When I'm not working, I'm doing this.' He opened his arms wide, gesturing to the cottage at large. 'Ongoing project.'

'Find anything new? Any more hexafoils?'

'Not lately.'

'Any visitors?'

'You're here.'

'Have you gone out?'

He lay back on the hardwood floor and looked up at the old beams that crossed the ceiling. 'Sure.' He'd waxed the floors himself, and the wood beneath his hands felt pleasing, so smooth it was almost soft, and he stroked it absentmindedly with his fingers.

'That's a no, then.' It was not a reprimand, but it wasn't a pardon either. She stood. 'I'm going to help myself to a glass of water. Would you like one?'

Eileen had started coming by as a favour to his mother, who was herself involved in the Church up in Whitley Bay and used this network to enlist Eileen; it was his mother's way of interfering without having to travel all the way to Norfolk. His mother often complained that he spent too much time shut away in 'that creepy old dump', that someone his age needed friends, needed to get out and do things. It was not that Arthur never left the cottage; he did, occasionally, when absolutely necessary, venture out for appointments or to collect groceries if all the delivery slots were full. His mother did not understand the nature of his introversion: that the very thought of leaving the cottage made him unwell, made him sweat and shake and sick to his stomach, an affliction that had steadily befallen him in the time he'd lived there.

That she'd taken it upon herself to send someone round to hang out with him, as if she were arranging a playdate, had been galling, particularly since the person she'd selected would have nothing in common with him (he couldn't think of someone more boring to spend his time with than a vicar), which showed, he thought, just how absurd his mother's concern was to begin with. He'd assumed this person would undoubtedly report back to her, and decided that when Eileen showed up on his doorstep that first afternoon and asked to be let in, he'd be polite enough but he'd also make it fun for himself and not be above antagonism, and before she'd even sat down, he told her that he was, unlike his mother, a staunch atheist and that he did not buy into the fire and brimstone propaganda; she'd surprised him completely when she said that, in fact, neither did she. As far as she was concerned, Hell, she said, was nothing more than a tool to control the masses. They talked at length on the government, on banned books and music today versus back-in-the-day. He found her fascinating and confounding in equal measure, so naturally he invited her back the following week, requesting that she keep it from his mother, and it had been that way ever since.

Eileen set two glasses of water on the floor between them and settled again in the chair, and the two of them lapsed into companionable silence. Arthur luxuriated in the peacefulness of outside, grateful that the commotion of cutting down the woods did not carry over to a Saturday. The development site was situated further along the river, but the noise carried and made it sound much closer, the discordant peal of chainsaws and shouting filling the rooms of his cottage unbearably when the windows were open. It had been that way for over two weeks now, the daylight hours disturbed since the tree surgeons had resumed clearing the woodland.

When Eileen spoke again, her voice was gentle. 'I thought we decided that you'd get some fresh air.'

'I get fresh air whenever I want.' He motioned to the window with his foot.

'Ha ha,' she said, sardonically.

A sudden dull squeal as they spoke, like a door swinging shut, made her turn sharply in her chair and scrutinise the empty room. She'd told him once there were stories that the cottage – which she'd said was actually the oldest surviving structure in Hesket, aside from the church – was supposedly haunted, but then he'd made some joke about the Holy Spirit, and she'd not brought it up since.

He stretched, languorous on the floor. 'Has your son left for Penzance?'

She turned again to the window. 'Mmm.'

'You must miss him.'

'Yes, well,' she said wearily. 'Apparently, he's already not getting on with his girlfriend, now that they're living together.' She pulled a face, her mouth exaggerated downward, a bit like a fish. 'Mo's going to see him next month.'

'That's a shame.'

The cottage windows were made of old glass that was wavy in parts, so that the world outside was as blurred as a dream after waking. From where he lay, he could see oak and willow crowns swooning across the river; the wind pulled a few leaves from the branches, so that indistinct pieces of gold skipped away beyond the frame of his view. They had done well to keep them this long after so little rain, sustained throughout the drought by their proximity to the river.

Eileen said quietly, 'If I lived here, I'd be very unproductive.'

That Eileen was a quarter of a century older than Arthur was not off-putting, nor was her religious faith or her intense dislike of *Die Hard*. He looked forward to his conversations with her, partly because they were not afraid to disagree and that made for interesting discussion, and partly because he liked to watch the way her lip curled around a particular crooked tooth when she talked, catching on the tapered point that jutted out.

'Listen.' She turned to him, her hands on the arm of the chair; she seemed suddenly charged with a self-conscious energy, and spoke quickly. 'I know you won't want to, but I've something to ask of you.'

Arthur sat up. 'Go on?'

'I'm having a party.' He saw that she was blushing. 'It's a birthday party. Dinner. It's all very frivolous.' She lowered her gaze and began to pick tiny bobbles off her jumper, collecting the fluff in her palm. He could imagine her then as a young woman: shy, but earnest and, in a way, passionate. 'Anyway, it's in eight days – on the twenty-first – and we've had someone drop out, which means there's a spare seat. You'd be doing me a favour if you came. So, what do you think?'

When she looked at him, it was with a kind of hopefulness, a desire, even, that he should say yes to her, and he was surprised to find it mirrored within himself. It was flattery he felt most of all, that she wanted him there, but also that she should unexpectedly become so nervous because of him. There was the sense that a new possibility had been opened up to him, and though he wasn't yet certain of what exactly it might be, it was in some way alluring. And since this event was to take place in the future and was of no immediate consequence to him now, he said, 'Of course I will.'

A long, stuttering creak came from the floorboards then, that juddered through him as the cottage shifted, intensifying when she put her hand on his wrist, rubbed his skin with her thumb. It was the first time so intimate a gesture had passed between them, and it shocked him that he discerned a certain pleasure from it.

'I can't tell you how much I appreciate it.' She smiled at him.

'Anything for you.' And because that sounded too fervent, he bowed exaggeratedly to make it seem less truthful, which was difficult to do while sat on the floor.

Emboldened by her bashfulness, he said, 'Will I be sat near you?'

The question appeared to catch her off-guard, if only momentarily. 'Well, I thought ...' she began. And then, 'Yes, if you'd like.'

'I would,' he said. 'Would you?'

She looked down at another bit of pilled fabric as she pulled it from her sleeve, and said tenderly, 'Course I would, Arthur.'

When she left, he sank into the lingering warmth of her empty armchair and watched the wind flurry the leaves outside, and as the cottage knocked and whined, he imagined for the first time Eileen sat at the little kitchen table of a morning with the paper spread out, reading choice bits aloud to him while he made them coffee on the stove, speckling the newsprint in ruby smudges of jam and crumbs of homemade bread.

The estate agent had described Filby Cottage as a little tired but full of character. Of all the houses Arthur had seen and could afford, this was the most neglected, the most unloved. That it had been abandoned for years had only intensified its disrepair. It was equal parts holey and clogged and loose and calcified and leaking and swollen and cracked and mouldy. But despite all of this, its bones were still good: the plumbing and electrical – added along with sash windows relatively late in its life, during the twentieth century – were miraculously still in fine working order; it had beautiful, if woodworm-infested, timeworn beams; the fireplace was large enough that he could walk into it if he stooped; outside, the exposed wattle and daub was mostly in good shape, white in some places, yellow-ochre where it had been replaced following a historic flood; within the wilderness of the garden were rambling roses, and it sat beside a river (a river! On the edge of a woodland, no less), and how many people could say they lived in a place that was like a cottage from a fairy tale? He had a decent enough sum of inheritance, and so he made an offer in the spirit of adventure and moved in not long after.

For money's sake, he took on the project himself, room by room in the spare hours between sleep and working from home. He was intensely content in the company of the cottage, happy to take a bleach solution to the mould and a bowl of vinegar to the limescaled taps, to replace its myriad broken tiles and spray woodworm treatment, patch and paint every wall. Sometimes he wondered when anyone had last cared for it like he did. As time passed, he was pleased with how comforting the cottage became, how warm and familiar and charming, and how lucky he was when the sun puddled like syrup on the hardwood in the afternoon.

The more time Arthur spent at home, the more he

understood there was a difference between being alone and loneliness. He did not feel alone.

Not ever.

For one thing, the cottage itself was constantly making noise, expanding and contracting according to the weather, the temperature, and its compact size gave it an intimacy and fullness, so that even though it was just him there, none of the rooms ever had the impression of being empty. It was a warren of chambers, one leading into another, and all of them very nearly too small for furniture. The ceiling lights were wired nearest the outer walls so that at night the rooms were all darker on one side. The floor in his makeshift office (which was just a cupboard he'd converted by installing a plank of wood for a desk) was terribly bowed, so that whenever he worked, he had to sit in his wheely chair with both feet planted or else he'd roll into the living room. The bathroom sink spouted only scalding water.

And then there were the multitude of unusual things that had for so long been hidden away from human eyes, disclosed to him over the months of his residency like so many little gifts: a crudely carved wooden horse about the dimensions of a tealight and hidden behind a baseboard, so *obviously* male (it was unrealistic, that size, certainly?!); a sliver-thin coin half-embedded in ceiling timber, snapped in two when he tried to dislodge it, so that one half was still wedged in the beam, the other he kept in his pocket, like two halves of a friendship token; a child's leather shoe beneath a loose floorboard, flattened and dusty and stiff; and there was an object made of plaited wheat stalks, nebulously shaped like a heart. And one afternoon, when the sun was low enough, it threw into relief carvings in the fireplace, intersecting lines roughly like a chequerboard and others that looked like encircled six-petalled flowers, and then he noticed more of them, etched into beams and across the top of the front door.

'They'll be hexafoils,' Eileen had said when he showed her. It was in the early days of her coming round. 'They were believed to provide protection from witches,' she explained enthusiastically. 'The idea was a witch would get trapped in them. I've found remnants of a few carved in some of the more ancient trees in Spry Wood; I suspect they were probably the hanging trees. There were witch-hunts here, you know. A lot of women were accused. A devastating amount, actually, if you consider the size of the village.'

'What happened to them?'

'Killed, God rest them.'

'I had no idea.'

'No,' she said. 'It's not exactly the kind of thing to boast about, is it? All those women tortured and then swum; that was how they were tested for being a witch, by dunking them into the river. If they sank, they were innocent, though of course they'd already drowned by that point. If they floated it meant they were rejected by God, so they were hanged. Doomed either way.'

'I thought witches were burned at the stake.'

'Not in England; Scotland and Europe, yes. But witchcraft was a felony here, so they were hanged. I don't think they were burned in Salem either, but the first person to be executed at the trials there was actually a woman from Norfolk – Norwich, I think. Bridget Bishop. You can impress people with that fact next time you're at a party.'

'I didn't know you were such a history buff.'

'Things shouldn't be forgotten just because they're unpleasant. I think there could at least be a plaque put up in the village, some acknowledgement those poor women existed, but the parish council favour the approach that it's best not to be haunted by such awful events from our past.' She sounded disapproving. 'It wasn't just old, lonely eccentrics who were killed, you know. There would've been women just like me.'

He raised his eyebrows.

She pressed her hand solemnly to her chest. 'I'm the first female vicar this parish has ever had and there were people spitting about it when I took the post, and that was in the *nineties*. I can't imagine an attempt at something so brazen would've gone over too well in those days, do you?'

And so that was how this odd little lump of earth and timber, after having been abandoned for so long before Arthur fixed it up and gave it new life, got another name: Hex Cottage, an homage to history not forgotten.

In the days since Eileen's visit, there had been a feeling that hung in the air like an unexpected change in barometric pressure, permeating every part of the cottage, so that he often had to open a window or turn on the television, or play music very loudly just to ease it: the constant sense of a presence just beyond the edge of his vision or in another room, as if at any moment a cough or a sigh might be heard, though of course there never was. It was worse at night when the tree surgeons were gone and every noise the old cottage made was magnified – a groan that would pull him from the edge of sleep, a loud pop like the cracking of a bone.

But he was too much in good spirits to be ill at ease. The promise of the invitation had buoyed him considerably. It seemed like a development in their relationship, a forward progression. He began to imagine her nervousness that day was because she was in some way attracted to him; whether she'd only realised it that afternoon or had harboured thoughts of him for a long time, both were entertained. These fantasies were intoxicating, and the more he dwelled on them, the more they intensified and grew, shapeshifting into a quiet lust or passionate sex, and sometimes even confessions of love; and the more, too, that he associated Eileen with attraction and sex and romance, the more he wondered if the reason he was entertaining these waking dreams so ardently was because he was recognising his own dawning longing for her. She was not an unattractive woman; he'd always found her eyes, which were deep set and blue, and her soft waves of pale, thick hair, to be striking. That she wanted him to meet her friends, who were themselves also likely to be older and perhaps worldly people, probably meant that she must think of him as having a similar maturity level. Her husband, Morris, never really factored as a complication – Arthur imagined him to be a dull, tedious man, dense to the interests and desires of his wife, disparaged and put-upwith by her friends, who all secretly thought him unequal to Eileen. He googled things like *famous couples with large age gaps* while he was meant to be working on the website design for a new client, spent long bouts of time imagining various hushed conversations with her at the upcoming party, in which she admitted to her infatuation with him.

In these periods of enthusiasm, he'd start to make preparations even though it was still days away: he carefully selected an outfit, which he ironed and hung on the back of his door; cleaned and polished his only pair of smart shoes; and as he cut his hair at the bathroom sink, he thought of a gift for her, a gesture that she would find touching, meaningful, something between the two of them.

He would bake her a loaf of soda bread.

He ran the clippers over his scalp and imagined presenting the bread to her, somewhere – probably in the kitchen – away from everyone else. She'd smile as she unwrapped the cloth it was nestled in, and gasp when she realised what it was. *Oh*, she'd whisper, *how thoughtful of you to remember,* and would insist that they share a piece, just the two of them, that it was too special to put out for everyone else to paw at. Closing her eyes, she'd bite into it, moaning softly. He'd place his hand on her arm – no, her lower back – and she'd angle her face to him, the shape of her breasts obvious beneath her blouse (he tried to imagine her in a low-cut dress, but couldn't visualise anything other than the modest blouses and jumpers she always wore). And then he would kiss her, passionately and against the fridge, so that her clerical collar sprung undone, her jutting tooth against his tongue.

He fantasised that the gentle scrape of the clippers at his neck were her impassioned fingernails. There was suddenly an awful clunking and screeching of pipes, as the tap spluttered surprisingly to life and began to gush so forcefully it sprayed the mirror and floor, and all over his torso, hot water that made the fabric of his T-shirt cling to his belly, and his trousers feel pleasurably warm against his thighs and groin.

As the days unfolded, he oscillated between excitement and trepidation. To leave the cottage was an unwelcome thought that made adrenalin knock through his body. But then, his mind would return to Eileen, to the invitation and what it could mean, to the stolen whispers and brushes of skin he'd imagined in those idle moments, and his desire to attend would dominate again.

He woke on Tuesday morning, three days before the party, slick with sweat. He pushed the duvet far from his naked body and found the sheets damp. The room was torrid, like he was in a greenhouse at the height of a summer afternoon. He put his hand to the radiator and found it was piping hot, even though the thermostat was set to zero. He fruitlessly wiggled the knob a bit, the dial refusing to turn; he would have to shut off the valve with a wrench. The air was sweltering, cloying, and made him nauseous. In the living room, he opened the window to let in some air, and pulled the armchair nearer so that he could sit with his face at the opening, breathing deeply the cool and gentle breeze, as it settled his stomach and wafted pleasantly against his feverish skin. Outside, the harsh cacophony of distant machinery was unpleasant, but there was something else too, closer and from above, the stiff sound of wood against wood, and then,

BANG.

The window slammed like a guillotine, less than an inch from his head. He recoiled jerkily into the armchair, hard enough that it fell backwards to the floor, and he lay for a few long moments on his back, heart thudding in his ears, until the relief that it had not come crashing on his skull swept over him like a euphoria.

This near fracturing of his cranium woke him up to the reality of what he'd agreed to do, and regret began to rise in him like a new dawn. It was bad enough he'd have to be sociable with people he'd never met, that they'd want to know who he was and what he did, why he was there at all, but worse still, he'd have to try to be someone interesting in front of the woman he now fancied. More than that, it was the leaving his home that caused an acute dread. He liked Hesket, had been drawn to its small, rural charms – the quaint ford where the river ran across the road, the encompassing countryside that promised beautiful walks – and yet, weirdly, he didn't step outside. There was nothing he could pinpoint about venturing out of the cottage that made him this way; he wasn't paranoid that something horrible would happen or that certain death waited for him. It was not logical, he knew, but seemed instead to come from some other place he couldn't locate, and influence him on a level beyond rational thought.

He'd not always been like this. Reclusive. Certainly, it wasn't that long ago he was in the pub of an evening with friends, was it, playing board games and drinking pints? Granted, he'd always had anxiety, social and otherwise, but not to this extent, not when he'd lived in Norwich, which had not been such an unreasonable distance away at the time. He'd assured his friends that nothing would change – it was, after all, an easy enough trip by bus, only thirty-five minutes – but everything these days felt too distant, too far away. When had he started making excuses? When had they stopped inviting him out?

Two days before the party, he woke to flakes of paint scattered across his pillow and in his hair like pale blue confetti. It was just above his bed, one long crack in the wall, the paint blistering off in patches to reveal a buttery yellow layer. The internet suggested the cause was damp, which made sense given the cottage's proximity to the river and its old single-glazed windows. He moved his bed as far from the wall as he could, which was not easy in a room so small, then pulled a fan from the jumble in his cupboard and turned it on high.

By the afternoon it was worse. The room resembled a snow globe, with scales of magnolia and off-white, a violent shade of crimson, billowing around as the fan huffed. There was now a patch larger than his head, and he rubbed the edge of it with his thumb, where the years of paint hollowed out in millimetres. Next came wallpaper, something floral that lifted at the seam and peeled away, and then citrus fruits, art deco shells hanging from the wall in scrolls, more paint, then florals again, a history revealed in sheets. The patch continued to spread, was now the size of a bread bin, and he pressed the back of his hand to it, was surprised by how dry it felt; if not damp, then what? He returned the fan to the cupboard.

The following day revealed lime plaster that was marbled in raised fissures. By the time Arthur was readying for bed that night – the night before Eileen's party – it had broken away in brittle scabs to reveal a lumpy daub, which Eileen had once told him was some various combination of clay, dung and sand, and likely included straw from Hesket's own meadow and soil from Spry Wood; there was a crude lattice of old wooden strips where small pieces of daub had broken off with the plaster. The patch now occupied a surface area larger than his computer monitor, having grown at an alarming rate. He turned out the light and climbed into bed, wondering what to do about it. Moonlight filtered through the curtain, the room shadowy but not completely dark. He hadn't lain there long before he heard it, a slow scraping that made his eardrums tingle in the stillness. He rolled over, trying to see, to pinpoint the sound. He looked at the wall, the patch reduced to a dark shadow.

There is something about night-time that intensifies a thought, a feeling, a sense.

Scraaaaaape.

A ripple of fear then.

Scraaaaaaaaaaape. Slow, methodical, as if taunting—

He was being ridiculous; he scoffed out loud to assure himself just how ridiculous he was being. It was the looming party that was getting to him, making him on edge like this. That's all it was. That and a rodent behind the daub. He could only hear it now because of everything that had fallen away, all those layers that had insulated any noise before. He rolled over, his back to the wall, and did his best to ignore it.

*

When he woke, he lay there for some long, groggy minutes in the faint light of morning, the weight of an unsettled sleep haunting the room like a dense fog. He rolled over and saw the wall, no longer a patch of exposed daub, but a hole, with splints of wood and rubble on the floor.

He got out of bed, cautiously moved closer to it.

At first, he couldn't quite tell what it was. Like hard, dried-out leather. Then he noticed the rows of yellowed, pointed teeth that were attached to a grotesquely shrivelled head, mouth agape as if in surprise, the empty pits for eye sockets. And then the strange, stiff contortion of its desiccated body, bones protruding through taut hairless skin, the hooked needle-like claws at the end of its withered legs, its thin, rattish tail. A cat, mummified, trapped in the wall. He'd heard of them being found in old houses, but having only lived in council estates and new-build flats until now, he'd never seen one for himself, nor had he known anyone who did. And to think it'd been there this whole time, only inches from his slumbering head, sealed inside an alcove of fretted wood, like a purposely made tomb.

The cat unnerved him. Since his discovery of it that morning, he'd done his best to avoid the bedroom altogether, but even so, morbid fascination had him periodically peering at its angular skull, the bony contortions of its body.

The soda bread was cooling on the kitchen table; he traced with his finger where the dough had cracked and split apart as it baked. He'd never made soda bread before, was worried it might be overdone, inedible, and that Eileen might say, pityingly, that it was a shame, and refuse to eat it.

By the time he was to leave, it was already dark out. He ran a cloth over his polished shoes again, carefully re-ironed his best shirt and trousers. He could not recall when he'd worn them last, the cotton crisp and pleasing on his body, and he felt quite good in them, attractive; he'd even found an old cologne, something musky and heavy. He put on his coat and wrapped the bread, pleasantly warm still, in a clean tea towel, and then he stood for a few moments, breathing deeply, preparing himself. Prolonged unease swirled strangely with the excitement of his fantasy potentially coming to life, and he retched in the toilet.

Returning home, hours later, he was intoxicated from the wine and good company, and from having left the house, properly, finally, for the first time in months. It was wonderful outside, the air brisk and vitalising. As he unlocked the door and stepped inside, he checked his phone, blearily, for the time. He squinted as he held it up to his face, and saw that it was probably too late – too early – to message his friends and suggest they meet at the Adam and Eve pub in Norwich on Sunday, but vowed to when the sun was up so that it wouldn't look like just a drunk text. It had been so long since he'd joined them for a roast, hadn't it? Why had he ever resigned himself to miserable hermitude? He made himself a cup of strong tea, giddy at having been out and social, felt invigorated in a way he hadn't for ages, even though the night did not go as he'd envisioned. To begin with, the bread had not been the magic apple he'd first hoped it would be. Eileen (who was dressed in a slightly more colourful variation of her usual jumper and slacks) put it out on the table, and he'd watched everyone help themselves; she'd not even managed a bite before it was gone completely. Actually, his romantic imaginings went entirely unfulfilled, hadn't even come close to being acted upon, and that he was indifferent about it surprised him. He leaned against the counter, taking small sips of hot, milky tea, and mulled over the alchemy of the evening.

The party had been a motley group of guests, mostly Eileen's age as he'd assumed, but one of them, Fiona, was the great-niece of a man in attendance and was perhaps several years younger than Arthur. She'd worn glasses and had curly hair, and shared self-deprecating anecdotes about singledom and dating in Norwich, which reminded Arthur about the things he'd neglected to include in his fantasies – jealousy, petty arguments, moods – and he realised (was even, admittedly, a little embarrassed at) how disconnected he'd been, holed up alone in the cottage for so long; he had no stories to contribute of his own, of course, not since he'd lived in Hesket.

He'd been preoccupied with Eileen's mouth over dinner, how it sprayed spittle when she laughed, and wet bits of food that clotted unappealingly around her protruding tooth, and he found himself repelled by it. It became clear as the night went on that he'd allowed himself to get carried away, that his solitary existence had swelled what should have only been a passing thought into some unwieldy obsession. He was not sure now that Eileen even thought of him in that way at all. In fact, it was entirely probable he'd misinterpreted her nervousness, that she'd not been anxious he would turn her down but was in fact sheepish for having to ask him in the first place, because his invitation was so clearly an afterthought; she'd said, didn't she, that someone else hadn't been able to go, that there was a spot which needed filling. He would go to bed relieved that she didn't think of him as anything more than a friend.

As he entered his bedroom, that same moody atmosphere from before seemed more concentrated now, compressing the room. He had the distinct sensation at the top of his neck and inside his ears of expecting a sound, like waiting for the clap of thunder in a lightning storm, but the cottage remained unsettlingly still. He went straight to the bed, turning on the lamp beside it. Fiona, who'd come from the city, had regaled the party about having recently attended a séance nearby (she was sure it was the same village ...), and so he'd volleyed back by bringing the cat up, and it had gone over well as a curiosity. You always find things, Eileen had said, and recounted eagerly to the other guests the objects he'd shown her. And it was true, he'd found a lot of remarkable things – the coin, the hexafoils – but there was something about this one that felt different, niggled uncomfortably at him.

In his periphery, he was aware of the cat's hollow eye sockets staring out at the room as he undressed, and allowed himself to look at it. It was simply the drink fooling him – blurring his vision, distorting what he saw – but in the dim light, he was certain something gleamed in its horrid little mouth.

Tentatively, he inserted his finger into it.

Inside, it was soft and moist, slippery. A tongue. His immediate feeling was one of revulsion, and he pulled his finger out instinctively, his skin scraping against the rounded tip of one of its fanged teeth. For a moment, all he could do was blink at it uncomprehendingly. Surely the tongue was not still alive. Surely that was impossible. But no matter how much he blinked and rubbed at his eyes, he could not unsee how much it glistened.

He hurriedly gathered the duvet around him and bolted downstairs. By the time he reached the last step, he was already doubting that it had been real; he was drunk, that was all. He turned on all the lights and splashed his face with cold water, drinking from the tap in hurried gulps. He settled, finally, in the armchair, still chastising himself for having been so silly, so quick to spook, and was thinking vaguely about attempting to sleep down there when he heard a skittering noise, as if hail were falling down the chimney.

He waited, squinting into the fireplace, seeing nothing but dark emptiness. When he heard it again, he found his phone and turned on the torch app. He crawled into the mouth of the chimney, twisting round so that he could shine the light upward into its felting of cobwebs and soot. Angled the way it was, he could only really see into it a few metres, but it was enough to find a horde of mummified cats with their jaws stretched open, all of them filled with those sharp little pointed teeth and frozen in a gruesome hiss, and in that precise moment Eileen's words resurfaced, *You always find things*, as it dawned on him why the first cat had so troubled him: he had not *found* it, the way he had the things under the floorboards or wedged in the beams, but rather it seemed to him, with a sobering and horrible clarity, that the cottage had shown it to him intentionally – a gift, or a threat?

Epilogue

A cumulonimbus, exceptionally large and anvil-shaped, 12,000 feet high and more than a mile wide, if one were to measure, gathered in the earliest hours of the morning to form an altogether impressive and portentous column above Hesket. The first tentative droplets landed on the delicate petals of a saffron crocus just as the dawn was approaching. A vicar, up before anyone else, her mind cluttered and fraught as she readied for the day ahead – a trip to the coast in the hopes she might track down a young woman and apologise, atoning for the regret that had been plaguing her – was the first to notice raindrops splatter the windowpane. And because it hadn't rained in so long, she traced them briefly with her finger against the glass, and peered out at the looming dark mass overhead as it began to empty itself over the village.

It was less a shower than a sudden and almighty downpour. A week's worth of rain fell in the first twenty minutes alone. Months of drought had left the ground hard as quartz, and the downpour soon engulfed the surface in pools of water. Within two hours the rainfall measured over five inches, and the storm drains overflowed in sinewy rapids, inundating the road, swelling around car tyres and over the pavement, sluicing the front paths of the houses, and all the while the rain was still battering ceaselessly down.

In what would prove to be an altogether pointless endeavour against the unstoppable resolve of Mother Nature, people began to prepare their homes when the water started lapping against doorsteps: stuffing towels across the thresholds, piling their belongings on high shelves and kitchen counters, mopping up the puddles that crept beneath the door. As it was, the rain was to make history as the heaviest that the county had ever seen and the most disastrous event in Hesket on record, worse even than the flood of 1647.

After nine inches of rainfall, the Wensum was a rushing torrent, and in its fury, it burst its banks and 400 million gallons of water poured into the adjoining meadow and woodland, sending a chipper truck hurtling into a lone riverside cottage that crumbled unceremoniously at its corner, so that most of the wall was carried away in the current.

From the ford, the river surged into the village, filling the houses and church with even more water. One woman, who later claimed to have had psychic visions of the flood in the days leading up to the disaster, retreated to the stairs and watched helplessly as her table and chairs began to float around the room.

The force of the flood swept away cars parked along the road and uprooted a loosely reinstated tree stump in a local garden, disinterring a centuries-old skeleton, its bones later found in the churchyard on top of a chainsaw.

A major incident was declared.

It was later determined that the substantial loss of woodland contributed to the magnitude of the disaster; all those trees sacrificed for the development, all those thousands of gallons a day no longer being drunk from the soil by their extensive root systems. Such was the concern that a deforested landscape would only encourage more flooding in the area, the development was finally deemed to be dead in the water, so to speak, and plans were made to move it elsewhere. Of course, they only need look to Old Hesket and what had happened so long ago for the cause of it all; that kind of past can haunt a place. Nine women condemned to death, eight of them sentenced to hang and decay, and what is death but a return of matter to the earth to be absorbed by other living organisms, the process of bodily decomposition releasing energy into the surrounding environment to be reclaimed by nature and reused again in a new form? But trauma has a way of curdling things, and all that anguish and fear upon death was infused into what remained – energy transformed into a curse, seeping into the land like a slow poison, infecting its surroundings, becoming one with the mycorrhizal network that webs beneath the surface. And there it remained for centuries, fermenting in the soil, mutating the way any contagion does, into something stronger and stranger, waiting, growing, listening, before the ground was broken open and the woods ripped out, and the blight was released to Hesket like spores on the wind.

When at last the rain eased, Hesket was changed: the road was now a river, six feet deep in places; ground-floor rooms had been transformed into subaquatic caverns; the church nave resembled a Gothic swimming pool with only its ornate pulpit visible, rising out of the water like a lighthouse; what was left of the woodland was now a swamp, the meadow a swelling lake.

People sought safety in the upper storeys and watched debris float by their windows – twigs and leaves, plastic plant pots, a copy of the *Norfolk Times*. One woman attempted to climb onto the roof of her home from a bedroom window, but she slipped and nearly fell into the water, and clambered back inside again, standing in her haste on beads of excrement on the carpet left by a leveret that was dozing, unconcerned, on the bed. Another man had the foresight to rescue his rowing boat as the water level rose, and he eased himself into it from the window as his sons watched on, determined that the three of them would row to the care home down the road and check on the residents (they'd only recently moved a poor woman to a flat on the ground floor), while they all awaited the arrival of the emergency services.

And an enormous fish, bound for near four hundred years to roam the river, at last had her chance to venture to all those places she had before only glimpsed from her watery realm. She wove in exaltation through woodland bracken and hawthorn, birch and ash and yew, her old friends the oaks, and out into the wide expanse of meadowland, liberation found in its edgelessness. And then on to the allotment, where rows of brassicas tickled her long pale underbelly, and she swam over purple jewels of flower, past a shed corner that gently scraped her flank before she navigated towards the row of houses, which were half-submerged like a string of floats in a sea.

A boy, now sat waiting at the bow of the rowing boat while his dad was occupied with aiding the cautious backwards descent of his older brother from a first-floor window, gazed around the strange and surreal sight of Hesket drowned, and was the only one in the chaos that day to see her gliding through the water. It had been a kingfisher darting by that caused the boy to look towards the allotment and see the approaching fin cutting through the water. He hadn't time to register fear or shock; there was only an immediate sensation of awe. Her smooth, glinting back broke the surface when she neared, as if she wanted him to see her passing right next to the boat, so unafraid and so close, that he might touch her if he were bold enough. He understood there was a graceful effortlessness to her movement, a beauty to the mottling of green-brown scales and elegant upward curve of her jaw, the muscular line of her body. She was the hugest fish he'd ever seen, double the length of the boat, her bony pointed head passing the bow before her tail had even neared. He felt the power of her as the boat lifted easily in her swell, and then she was gone, up the village road and submerged again.

Acknowledgements

It takes a village to write about one.

I am so grateful to Alice Lutyens, who saw something in this book and took me on – thank you for your steadfast enthusiasm, story advice, and for always telling it like it is. Thank you also to Rakhi Kohli and the wonderful team at Curtis Brown, and to Olivia Bignold for your perceptive notes.

Sincere thanks to James Gurbutt for having confidence in me, giving Hesket a home, and helping to make it a truer place. To publicity whizz Lucy Martin, and to Alice Watkin, Alison Tulett, and everyone at Little, Brown who has had a hand in making this book something I can hold.

I am so appreciative to the people who've taken the time to read parts – if not all – of this book at its various stages over the years and offered their invaluable feedback. Naomi Wood, for all of your guidance (both writing and life) while I was at UEA, and for believing I could get this written when I felt it was an impossible task. And Nonia Williams, whose warmth and encouragement helped me get there in the end. To Gemma Barry, Emily Coutts, Louise Lamb, James Smart, Olivia Spidel, Kate Vine and Bridget Walsh – I have learned to be a more competent writer from each of you, and I appreciate it beyond measure. And my MA creative writing cohort of 2018, who are the warmest, most supportive, intimidatingly talented bunch I've had the pleasure to know.

This couldn't have been written without bolstering words along the way, and for those I thank many of the above, as well as Rick Bland, Laura Bridges, Andrew Cowan, Marina McClintock, Joe Hedinger, Amber Higgins, Phil and Mary Hunt, Tom Hunt, James Jones, Leanne Kramer, Louis Laurence, Annie MacGuffie, Cara Marks, Lucy McCarthy, Rich McLay, Ellie and Ollie Mills, Siobhan O'Donnell, Hale Öztekin-Cuss, Emily Owen, Kila Panaretou, Amy Salvatore, Jon Warren, Micky Willingale and Katherine Wood; morale-boosters, all of you. And to Nieve, Joan and Ari for being the most brilliant little pals when I needed to get out of my own head.

To my parents: Aemon – who has always told me stories – and June – who has always encouraged mine and kept every scrap I've written since I was a little girl – thank you for supporting me in all senses of the word. I love you very very very very very very much. With love to my brilliant brothers, Alex and Eamon – I have no doubt that all those childhood hours immersed in games of our own invention sparked the writing itch in me. And to my husband, Ben – sounding board, keen-eyed editor, map-drawer, patient re-reader – your unwavering belief in me and my childhood dream is staggering. Thank you for all the cups of warm comfort, my love.

RAISING READERS
Books Build Bright Futures

Dear Reader,

We'd love your attention for one more page to tell you about the crisis in children's reading, and what we can all do.

Studies have shown that reading for fun is the **single biggest predictor of a child's future life chances** – more than family circumstance, parents' educational background or income. It improves academic results, mental health, wealth, communication skills, ambition and happiness.[1]

The number of children reading for fun is in rapid decline. Young people have a lot of competition for their time. In 2024, 1 in 10 children and young people in the UK aged 5 to 18 did not own a single book at home.[2]

Hachette works extensively with schools, libraries and literacy charities, but here are some ways we can all raise more readers:

- Reading to children for just 10 minutes a day makes a difference
- Don't give up if children aren't regular readers – there will be books for them!
- Visit bookshops and libraries to get recommendations
- Encourage them to listen to audiobooks
- Support school libraries
- Give books as gifts

There's a lot more information about how to encourage children to read on our website: **www.RaisingReaders.co.uk**

Thank you for reading.

---

[1] OECD, '21st-Century Readers: Developing Literacy Skills in a Digital World', 2021, https://www.oecd.org/en/publications/21st-century-readers_a83d84cb-en.html

[2] National Literacy Trust, 'Book Ownership in 2024', November 2024, https://literacytrust.org.uk/research-services/research-reports/book-ownership-in-2024